D1201130

Bitter
A Novel
Bitch

Bitter Bitch

A Novel

Maria Sveland

Translated by
Katarina E. Tucker

A Herman Graf Book
Skyhorse Publishing

Skyhorse Publishing books may be purchased in bulk at special discounts
for sales promotion, corporate gifts, fund-raising, or educational purposes.
Special editions can also be created to specifications. For details, contact
the Special Sales Department, Skyhorse Publishing, 307 West 36th Street,
11th Floor, New York, NY 10018 or info@skyhorsepublishing.com.

www.skyhorsepublishing.com

10 9 8 7 6 5 4 3 2 1

Library of Congress Cataloging-in-Publication Data is available on file

PEFC
PEFC/16-33-111
CATG-PEFC-052
www.pefc.org

For Olof, Leo and Max

JOY OF FLYING

It is a hideous January morning and I am sitting on a plane to Tenerife. I feel so bloody tired, so hideous, and so damned angry; no not angry, *irritated*. I am so damned irritated at everything, but mostly at myself, and I feel ice-cold inside. I have been angry for a long time, and the anger is like a solid grey mass that makes me stiff, makes me want to drink too much wine and forget everything hideous – like January mornings.

I have always hated January.

I am sitting here on the plane reading *Fear of Flying*, trying to get myself in a good mood, maybe even to feel downright happy for a little while.

I am only thirty years old, but boy am I bitter. I'm a real bitter bitch, a bitter cunt, in fact.

It was not supposed to be this way. Like everyone, I dreamed of love, but a suspicion, an insight, has started to grow inside me, forming a deep, festering wound: *How will we ever achieve an equal society if we can't even live in equality with those whom we love?*

I am thirty, just like Isadora in *Fear of Flying*, but I am infinitely more tired, more mundane. Family hell, with all of its sordid

1

emotional stains, has drained me of energy. I could be her. I could be you, Isadora, if I were able to feel more, but I am disconnected from everything and I am not even afraid of flying. And I do not know how I will survive without bitterness when there are so many reasons to be bitter. All of the women you see, with their cheerless expressions and empty eyes, the ones who snap at you to get out of the way in the dairy aisle, making you want to snap back: *witch*. They make you angry for the rest of the day, don't they – but is that because they remind you of someone?

I was struck the other day by the revelation that I run the risk of ending up just like one of them in twenty years' time. I am already halfway through my bitter bitch cunt transformation, which seems impossible to avoid when we live in a society that discriminates, rapes, abuses and violates girls and women. But every time I see a cheerless old hag, I tell myself that deep down inside there is a happy little girl who once dreamed magnificent dreams without boundaries.

I am sitting here on the plane reading my book about Isadora. She is on her way to a psychoanalytical conference in Vienna, together with 117 psychoanalysts and her psychoanalyst husband, Bennett.

There are not 117 psychoanalysts on my plane, just me and sixty or so other sallow January wretches who appear to be in varying states of unhappiness. Nor am I on my way to the Congress of Dreams or a glorious fuck with some wonderful stranger, just a spa hotel built in the 1980s which will probably be occupied by retirees, the odd young family, and me. But then everything was so amazingly carefree in the 1970s when Erica Jong wrote *Fear of Flying*, and that is partly why I am sitting here, a bitter bitch.

While she got to fuck around, undergo analysis, do drugs, be left wing and part of a big fat women's movement, I grew up and became a teenager during the fearful, anti-feminist 1980s when everything was dark blue, even the mascara.

Erica Jong coined the concept *the zipless fuck* – the pure, guilt-free encounter, a fuck free of emotional baggage and remorse, free of power struggles. But that was then, during the carefree 1970s. Thirty years later, we are in a completely different world. I have coined the expression *bitter bitch* to describe us: laden with guilt and filled with all of history's injustices, weighed down by the battle of the sexes. What you become in this society – if you are a woman.

Isadora preached zipless fucks and drugs; my generation received lectures on AIDS and drug abuse. When we got older, and sought therapy, the queues were endless because weakness doesn't fit into the free market's myth of success; and then, just when we were ready to seek employment, Sweden found itself in a recession so deep that the unemployment rate was no joke.

And then one day it is January and I am sitting on a plane reading about Isadora's zipless fuck, and about Bennett and Adrian, her husband and her lover. I am sitting on a plane on my way to Tame Tenerife instead of zipless fucking at a psychoanalytical conference in Vienna.

A couple in their thirties is sitting next to me and as I get out my book, I hear the woman begin to sob. She has her face to the tiny window and her shoulders are shaking. Her boyfriend, clean cut and dressed in a suit, sees that I see. He points at my book and rolls his eyes.

'You'll have to excuse my girlfriend, she's afraid of flying. Maybe she should read your book,' he says, and attempts a laugh, but it catches in his throat and just sounds mean.

'I don't understand why you're afraid. Did you know that travelling by car is more dangerous than flying?!'

He looks at me again, searching for support, but I stare at my book. She turns towards him and sobs against his shoulder.

'I know. It's stupid but I can't help it.'

The stewardess comes over, an older woman with a large, comforting bosom. She leans forward and speaks, her lips carefully painted pink. She has a calming stewardess voice and kind eyes that meet those of Fear of Flying Girl.

'Do you want to come up to the cockpit and have a look?' the stewardess asks, covering us with her dry, old lady perfume. I like her. I think Fear of Flying Girl likes her too, happy that someone is trying to comfort her instead of mocking.

'No, thanks. I don't think so. It usually passes as soon as we're up in the air. It's worse during take-off and landing.'

'Yes, that's what it's like for most people,' the stewardess replies. 'Shall I get you a drink?'

'Yes, please. Thanks so much!' Fear of Flying Girl looks up at her guardian angel gratefully. Her boyfriend is sitting quietly and seems to think the whole thing is embarrassing. A *scene*. We are flying high and my ears are buzzing. I am glad we are in the air now.

The stewardess voice over the loudspeaker is soft. We're sooo welcome and she hopes we'll have a pleasant flight. And just think, today is the day she has *fantastic* deals, for everyone.

'Gucci perfume for just 100 kronor. Or why not three mascaras that'll make your eyelashes long, black and beautiful. All at very attractive prices.'

I do not know when poor stewardesses were forced to start working as sales people, but Fear of Flying Girl buys the mascara and her boyfriend continues to brood quietly rather than comfort her.

Breakfast is served, and as I eat I feel the tiredness disappear along with the sweet yoghurt, warm cheese sandwich and black coffee. Either the breakfast or the whisky has calmed Fear of Flying Girl because she has stopped crying and wants to talk.

'Aren't you ever afraid of flying?' she asks me.

'Nope, but I'm afraid of a lot of other things!' I answer. I do not want her to feel stupid and in any case it's true. I am ter-rified of all sorts of things: walking home alone from the train station at night, travelling by car, biking, not being loved.

She asks if I am travelling alone and when I answer yes she gives me a wide-eyed look.

'God you're brave, I could never do that!'

It makes me happy to know there is someone who thinks I am brave, even a girl who is afraid of flying. I smile and tell her that I am sleep deprived because of my two-year-old son and need a little break from it all.

'His name is Sigge. Want to see a picture?' I ask, and proudly show her the photograph I always carry with me. A trophy and a reminder, because I cannot deny that my daydreams are increas-ingly about a vast, unrestricted solitude, one without husband and child, the kind of quiet solitude that makes room for think-ing. Daydreams that fill me with endless guilt and isolation.

I realize that I need to explain that I am normal and have a family, but if anything this has the opposite effect on Fear of Flying Girl. I go from being brave for travelling alone to being suspect.

'But isn't your son going to miss you?'

'Yes, and I'm going to miss him, but I think I will be a better mother if I get to rest this week.'

Fear of Flying Girl looks at me through narrowed eyes.

'It's really just one week,' I plead, but she is ruthless.

'But isn't a week a long time for a two year old?'

'Yes,' I say.

Fear of Flying Girl squeezes her boyfriend's hand and kisses him on the cheek. He looks up from his magazine and kisses her back. They look at each other in loving understanding.

It was not until I told my friends and family that I was leaving my husband and son for a week without a valid reason that I understood that it was weird. 'Are you and Johan having problems?' most of them asked, and maybe we were. After intense touring around family and friends in Västerås during the holidays, the passion level in January was so-so, but no worse than usual, no marital crisis or anything, just a slightly abnormal tiredness combined with the logistical nightmare of having a toddler and two demanding careers on which we are both dangerously dependent.

Then it is suddenly there when you wake, an abyss that opens up on a dark January morning, for example, a bottomless fatigue. I looked out across the snow-covered roofs and registered dryly that it was beautiful. A wonderland. For a brief moment I felt a spark, but the sensation soon transformed itself into an objective statement.

Where did the sparks go? I looked at my husband eating breakfast across from me. He was reading the sports section with the same detachment with which I was reading the arts one. I tried listening to the radio, but they were only words and I wished I listened to music in the morning. Wished I was someone who drank tea instead of disgusting coffee, ate my breakfast on the sofa, listened to classical music and thought. But the coffee was poisonous and the radio disturbing and something about it all was appealing; some quality that matched the feeling of numbness.

Sigge was playing in his room and I thought with irritation of the stress of soon making my way through the slush to daycare and then on to the train, which would be packed and damp with its steamy windows.

Always stressed, always tired and often irritable. My hair would get wet because I had left my hat at the paper the day before and I knew I would freeze, and I hated January. Immensely.

Sometimes the pain was so intense I had to pretend I was part of a movie, playing a role: emotionless young mother posing on the sofa in a Chinese robe. Maybe I was beautiful?

Our wedding photo hangs in the hall like a taunting reminder of everything we dreamed of, everything we wanted. It rained the entire day and so I got married in a yellow raincoat.

When I stare at the picture I see my puffy eyes and my wet hair plastered to one side of my head. I was crying, moved by all the thoughtfulness, the care and the warmth we had received from our friends and family.

Getting married felt so amazing and adult and beautiful, but I was forced to start joking about the absurdity of it all only a few months later, the fact that I had gone and got married. It is not that I do not love Johan, I always have (with the exception of a year-long marital crisis), but the truth is that I can't answer for being married. I cannot stand the shitty baggage that goes with marriage. The acrid taste in your mouth when you think about what marriage stands for: hundreds of years of oppression and millions of unhappy people hissing in the background. I do not know how to handle my conflicting feelings, of wanting to be married even though I do not know of a single happy marriage. It is like having a blister on your tongue you are forced to touch even though it stings. I cannot stop reading all the books which criticize marriage, especially the ones from the 1970s.

That is why I read *Fear of Flying* over and over again, that is why I devour Denmark's Erica Jong, Suzanne Brøgger, reading her desperation regarding the nuclear family as if it were my own, and then realize that it is my own.

I do not know of any happy families or marriages, none, not even among those closest to me: grandmothers, grandfathers, Mum, Dad, uncles or aunts, friends. Everyone is unhappily married, everyone is deceived by the myth of love.

My own poor head is stuffed with false love.

A Lill-Babs lives inside me. A Sue Ellen from the TV programme *Dallas*, with a pouty mouth and lips that tremble every time JR disappoints her. Lill-Babs, Swedish singer and actress, and Sue Ellen are tired, boring and rather sad but never angry. They sip on champagne and become just tipsy enough to hiss: I hate you, but softly, so that JR doesn't hear. My poor head is filled with images that stifle every drop of real emotion. These images of how love ought to taste make it difficult to tell if it is bitter, or salty, or sweet. In the beginning love is romantic, comprised of hilarious and exciting encounters and mix-ups, filled with desire. But then everything becomes quiet and you struggle desperately for it still to seem sacred and wonderful. And no one, not even your closest friends, talk about the pain. The real pain, not to be confused with the false grumbling women sometimes indulge in together. That superficial communion about how hopeless their men are, while these women keep cooking, cleaning and taking the children to daycare. A whine that may be an expression of the real pain beneath the surface that smoulders and causes cancer, but lacks the power to stoke the anger and achieve real change. A whine that is little more than a small whisper, leading women to continue to neglect their own lives and intellects, and devote everything to their husbands.

Real pain makes you wonder if you would have been happier had you chosen another kind of life. It makes you wonder if something is wrong with you, if you missed out on something everyone else has. Until you realize that the thundering silence is borne of everyone around you being completely engrossed in fostering their own lies about love.

I would like to understand what Suzanne Brøgger really means when she writes:

> Marital problems originate from the moment when love began to force its way into the family; which was not at all the idea. As a result, misery.

Maybe it was easier when marriage was built on reason, a business arrangement between friends? All romanticized expectations were avoided, but when romance and the myth of love came into the picture and took a patent on the couple, disappointment entered the picture too. Maybe that is when free love was kidnapped, reduced to something that should only apply to two, man and woman. Coupling, writes Brøgger, is an organized form of an unlived life. *A string of non-meetings.* Her words are almost the most beautiful thing I have ever read.

If only I were a member of a church, a foolishly happy wife and mother. It is devastating to have a self-image which revolves around my lifestyle in 1994, before I met Johan; all the parties, the men, the time, the sleep, the freedom. It is just as devastating as constantly daydreaming about the 1970s. When the tension between daydream and reality becomes too great, you start to become a bitter bitch. I try to fight it but there are a lot of reasons that cannot be overlooked, all of which lead me to make bitter bitch analyses, all the conspiratorial facts I read and hear which confirm what I already suspect. Besides, it is January and I am thirty, a young mother and I have been married for seven years. Seven years! And everything is so disconnected. And I hate January so much.

The only thing that helps for a while is a warm bath. I have lowered my body into hot bath-water every night for four weeks now. The water consoles and encloses, makes me warm and weightless and delightfully giddy. I can lock myself in the bathroom and refuse to answer when I am spoken to. In the bathtub I have read and comforted myself with Isadora's longing.

> Those longings to hit the open road from time to time, to discover whether you could still live alone inside your own head, to discover whether you could manage to survive in a cabin in the woods without going mad; to discover, in short, whether you were still whole after so many years of being half of something . . . Five years of marriage had made me itchy for all those things: itchy for men, and itchy for solitude. Itchy for sex and itchy for the life of a recluse. I knew my itches were contradictory – and that made things even worse.

In the bathtub I read and I thought how I loved Isadora and her confusion, but I did not want to fuck, or have an affair with some other unhappy fool. Not even that. Even my daydreams are about solitude and time. Let me sleep and think endless thoughts.

One day last week my January life quite simply became unbearable. On Thursday morning I was in a hurry and cycled quickly, arriving at the Psychotherapy Clinic all sweaty. I was a few minutes late and annoyed because the woman at reception did not have change for a hundred. They never have change, as if they do not want to admit they accept payment. I tried drying myself off using the coarse paper towels they have in the loo, but it did not help because I was still sweating. I knew that therapist Niklas was waiting and as I had often done before, I began to cry. I do not know how many times I have stood there feeling sorry for myself. There is something about Niklas that evokes a great sadness in me, an invitation to be small and pitiful, knowing that he is still there, welcoming me. The kind big brother, a male relationship which for once is not filled with confused desire.

So I sat there across from him bemoaning January mornings, sleep deprivation and the fact that there were no more sparks. I cursed the emptiness and swore how much I longed to just run away.

He looked at me with those kind eyes I like so much. 'What's stopping you?'

I looked at him and could not answer. What was stopping me? Nothing really, not my job, not my husband, not the money. My hesitation was because of something completely different, something unspoken, a forbidden feeling, as if I was committing a horrible, criminal act. When I could not tell him what was actually stopping me, I became so annoyed that I started looking for trips that same night.

I did not want to go far away because I am too much of a coward and my longing for sun and warmth was too great to choose a bustling city. So it became a package holiday to Tenerife, a destination which matches the lame fool that I am. Or have become.

'I have to,' I explained to Johan, who admittedly did not stop me but was hardly overjoyed.

'It'll work wonders for our marriage. I'll come back a new person,' I continued. I needed his blessing to go, even if it was only for a petty week-long package holiday to Tenerife. Running off alone without my husband and child already felt taboo enough as it was.

I dreaded Sigge's punishment, him turning away, his eyes refusing to meet mine. Despite Johan having been away twenty times more than me since Sigge was born, Sigge was simply angry whenever I went away. Johan could be gone for weeks and Sigge missed him, affectionately and generously. He would throw himself in Johan's arms and seem overjoyed to see him. The few times I was gone more than one night it could take hours before Sigge stopped ignoring me. He had a cold determination that scared me and made me feel even more guilty. I asked Johan once if he knew why Sigge reacted that way. He answered quickly and simply.

'I have a clear conscience when I'm gone, but you feel so guilty it almost makes you sick. He senses your guilt and it confirms that he's right to be angry at you.'

I stood quietly for a long time, staring blankly. So damned obvious. The strange thing is that my whole life, the whole world, is filled with this kind of confusing paradox. And I try not to feel such guilt but it is buried fast, deep and unreachable.

Everything was open at Arlanda Airport and people, including myself, were wandering around in the shops, buying perfume, booze and sweets even though it was only five-thirty in the morning. For a while I thought about sitting down with the men in The Swedish Vodka Bar and ordering a vodka with ice, getting drunk and pretending I was urbane and single instead of a married, sleep-deprived young mother. But the magazines and mineral water in Pressbyrån were more appealing.

I am constantly reminded about everything I do not feel, everything I do not want. I think about Isadora and wonder what it would be like to be a little more like her, a little more interested in everyone, even if it creates more guilt and anxiety. Better anxiety than this nothingness. Isadora leers at strange men, stares at the bulge in their trousers and fantasizes about what they are like in bed. She sits on a train and fucks the man across from her with her eyes, she is filled with guilt but still wonderfully aroused.

> But what about all those other longings, which after
> a while marriage did nothing much to appease?

I do not know. All I know is that I have too much longing shooting off in every possible direction. A longing so immense that it has isolated me completely.

I stood there in Pressbyrån looking at the magazines until I realized I would be unhappy no matter which magazine I chose. I saw how they screamed deplorable messages about beauty, ugliness, weight, weight and weight. I noted that there was nothing similar among the men's sports and car magazines, and felt that familiar sting of jealousy, which was slowly and completely transforming me into a bitter bitch. At least four different bridal magazines were crammed together on the stand. I desperately wished it was 1975 instead of 2005. Wished that my name was Isadora and I was a free woman in New York instead of a boring mother from Stockholm, or at least a career woman with a clear conscience.

We are quite simply deceived. Something confirmed by a magazine queen I once interviewed. She had started several successful women's magazines and adorned the cover with her image as well as her name, and over a bowl of pasta with chanterelles she happily told me how carefree the 1970s had been.

'We didn't pay much attention to weight and things like that. We hardly knew what cellulite was.' She did not understand why I was so upset and I think she used the word bitter about me as she defended the content of her magazines.

'Why are you so bitter?'

In a way it was fantastic. This woman who, through her magazines, is informing an entire generation of Swedish women about cellulite, and how to get rid of it while losing twenty pounds, was explaining how much more fun it was during the 1970s when they did not have to think about it.

Yeah, we are definitely bitter. I am in any case. I did not buy a magazine, after all I had my Isadora Afraid to Fly. At least she makes me laugh.

I am listening to Nina Simone and the captain has just informed us that we are several thousand metres up in the air and the thought of the solitude that awaits me makes me grin. I am definitely not bitter to the core. Despite everything, I am making a small part of my daydreams of solitude and sleep into reality.

At the same time, my conscience, all the old taboos, are gnawing away at me. Why are egoistical women regarded as terribly provocative, while egoistical men are, if anything, seen as a given? Maybe it has something to do with the fact that our culture's religion begins with a raped woman?

A completely self-sacrificing woman, whose lack of ego the Christian Church urges us to worship. Even if you prefer not to literally interpret the conception as a rape, but to focus on the symbolism of a holy spirit impregnating her, how terrified must she have been? She was just a young teenager when she got knocked up with Jesus.

Not even Rosemary can stop loving her Satan child in Roman Polanski's *Rosemary's Baby*. She becomes pregnant after her husband enters into a pact with their devil-worshipping neighbours. Her husband lets Satan knock her up when she is drugged one night – an inverted version of the Jesus story, but with an unholy spirit. She feels terrible throughout the entire pregnancy and suspects a conspiracy without being able to find any proof. When she finally realizes what has happened, it is too late and she has an agonizing delivery. Yet despite everything her maternal instinct takes over when she wakes up. She is drawn to the child against her will even though she knows that her baby is Satan's son, with red eyes. Roman, the neighbour who is the brains behind the conspiracy, eagerly urges her to go and see her son. Rosemary hesitates, afraid of what she is going to see.

'You're trying to make me be his mother!' Rosemary says to Roman.

'Aren't you his mother?' he asks. Yes. It ends with Rosemary picking up the crying child and comforting him. She is his mother.

Jesus-child or Satan-child, obviously most of us love our children intensely, an emotion so strong it binds us to them for life. Even women who have become pregnant as a result of rape often have an unbelievable ability to love their children.

I just wish I was allowed to love in the same free way as men. The knowledge of how guilt-laden the maternal role is, how taken for granted and demanding it is when compared to that of the father, makes me a jealous bitter bitch. I want to be a man and have society applaud when I only use two months of my parental leave, while no one raises an eyebrow when my wife takes out the rest. I want to be a man and experience society applauding my love and my sacrifice as something fantastic, extraordinary. I wish I could love my child and still foster pure, egoistical feelings, like dreaming about sleep, solitude, sun and Tenerife.

They have started showing a movie but Fear of Flying Girl is sleeping soundly against her boyfriend's shoulder. I hear someone behind me hiss, 'For Christ's sake would you stop it!'

A woman replies inaudibly with a soft, ashamed voice. I am the only one who is travelling alone. Everyone else is together, mostly families and couples and a few who seem to be colleagues. This morning, when I was buying tickets for the airport train, the cashier told me the tickets were half price if I was travelling with someone else.

'Do you have to be travelling together?' I asked.

A stupid question, obviously they cannot check if you are in a relationship or not.

But I got the point when the cashier said that if I wanted to ask a stranger to buy tickets with me that was fine.

'But then you'll have to sit together on the train!'

When you live with someone you rarely think about the fact that society is built around couples. All the thousands of tiny signals. For example, there is always an advertisement for herpes ointment on the personal pages in the newspaper, such a nasty, self-righteous, sad reminder to all singles who are hungering after love.

My sense of thrift took over, and besides, I wanted to challenge this kind of madness. So I started looking for a suitable person, but there were few people on the Arlanda Express at five in the morning.

Finally I saw a man my own age and I walked over, even though he had a self-satisfied grin on his face, the type who thinks he is good looking. I started grinning too because I suddenly remembered a boy with learning difficulties Sigge and I met in the park during the summer. He was sitting on the swing next to Sigge's even though he was too big. He was swinging, and he looked at me and said, 'There she is wearing a green dress thinking she's so wonderful.' I was wearing a green dress and I thought I looked pretty wonderful in it. It was so fantastic that someone saw through me.

Of course pretty boy took my smile as an invitation and I wished I had learning difficulties so I could say, 'There he is in his suit thinking he's so wonderful.'

But instead I smiled sweetly and asked him if he wanted to buy a ticket with me and of course he said yes. Why can't I act the way I really want to? On Tuesday, when I was deciding between a red bikini and a sportier military green model for my holiday, I chose the sporty one. I did not want to send the wrong signal. I wanted to be left alone and escape this accursed game!

Pretty boy grinned the whole way to the airport and happily chatted about the weather in Sri Lanka and wanted to know where I was going and if I was travelling alone, and instead of engaging with him I just sat there and grinned and said yes, I am travelling alone. And I do not know why, but I think it is because I was foolish and sweet when I was fourteen, with a delightfully sick reflex: a treacherous fourteen-year-old's longing to be adored.

POPCORN AT NIGHT
(1982)

I do not know what my first image of love was, but I'm quite clear about what it *doesn't* look like: when love becomes distorted and ugly, when Dad yells awful things at Mum. I am sitting on the stairs and I can see her standing in the kitchen, her back to me. She does not answer him, instead she continues doing the dishes and his voice sounds strange, a Daddy voice that scares me. I go to my room and arrange things so that my dolls can sleep by my feet at the foot of the bed.

The dolls are my orphan children and I am their kind, pretend Mummy. There is no Daddy. I pull the covers over them and tuck them in so they will not freeze. My little sister is sleeping in the bed next to mine. I close the bedroom door so she will not wake up. Dad's angry voice has grown quiet. I do not know what they are doing. When I wake up the next morning, I hear Dad snoring from their bedroom. Mum is cleaning, up in the kitchen and from the stairs I can see her, back to me in the same place as last night, as if she has been standing there the whole night. But she couldn't have been, could she?

She is wiping off the counter and when I get closer I see that the cooker, the tiles, the counter, everything is smeared with butter. Dad has done it during one of his drunken rampages. Mum is crying and wiping. I want to comfort her and so I pat her on the back. I try to hug her, but she shakes her head and sets out breakfast.

When I am little, Dad is the one who knows the name of a Japanese fish so poisonous that one tiny piece killed hundreds of restaurant goers. Then Mum is angry when I won't eat fish for several months. Dad does not get angry, he laughs and says there are no fish like that in Sweden. But I have learned not to be sure of anything and I continue to refuse to eat fish.

Dad also knows how to make reservations at a luxury hotel in Stockholm where we go on holiday one weekend during the summer. He drives us there in his new Audi at 140 kilometres an hour. I throw up several times on the way and Mum asks him not to drive so fast. Dad gets irritable and Mum is already cross. She and I trade places so that I can sit in the front seat. Then my little sister gets tetchy because she does not get to sit in the front seat and then Dad gets really angry and tells all of us to shut up.

We sit quietly and Dad drives dangerously fast and I try to listen to the radio. Carola is singing about 'Tokyo' and 'Hey Mickey'.

When I am little, my father is the one who knows how to order at luxury restaurants, always fillet of beef with Béarnaise sauce which we agree does not taste nearly as good as the one he makes at home sometimes on Fridays. My Dad also knows why Olof Palme is a shit and why you should vote for the moderates. He says he wants to keep his money. When he gives us our money for sweets on Saturdays he pulls out a thick wad of hundreds which he flips through in front of the lady in the sweet shop.

'Unfortunately I don't have any smaller notes, I hope this is OK!' he says, and holds out one of the notes.

When I am little my father is the one who can buy almost anything, and for several years I want a real Barbie house but I never get one. Instead I build a house for one of my Barbie dolls in one of the drawers under my bed. Books become walls and I make a stove out of wrapping paper. Barbie and Ken fight a lot. Barbie is not sure that Ken loves her at all.

But he does. He loves her more than anything else in the world and he does not understand why Barbie thinks he does not love her. Then Barbie is so happy, so happy and they have sex and more sex until Mum calls that it's time to come and eat. She serves sausages and boiled potatoes. I say that it is not nearly as good as Dad's fillet of beef and Mum gets irritated and says that you cannot have fillet of beef every day.

When I am little my father is the one who comes home on Fridays after having been gone all week, working. He makes fillet of beef and Béarnaise sauce and we eat together by candlelight and Mum and Dad drink red wine. For about an hour, between seven and eight, we are a pretty happy family.

When I am little, my father is the one who has his own business with its own business cards. He travels around Sweden insulating buildings such as barns. The insulation foam is yellow and about as hard as Styrofoam, and Dad tells me and my sister Kajsa that was the sort of stuff they used to build the fortress in the film *Ronia the Robber's Daughter*, and that he and his partner came close to getting the job, but they did not get it, and he travels and travels and he is often gone two or three weeks at a time.

He is tired and sleeps a lot at the weekend. Mum is the one who gets up in the mornings and sets out breakfast, on weekends, weekdays, summer holidays and at Christmas time. Kajsa and I try to wake him up by jumping around on the bed yelling, 'Dad! Wake up Dad! Wake up! Wake up!' But he does not, and we continue dancing around on the bed where he lies like a beached whale. We sing, 'Fart Daddy, Wake up tooter! Wake up, wake up, wake up now you pee-pee head!' But he just grunts and turns over and keeps sleeping his heavy sleep, which is filled with snores.

We finally give up and go and play with our dolls. When Mum yells that lunch is ready, Dad finally wakes up and we nag him during lunch to build us a *Ronia the Robber's Daughter* fortress on the small lawn at the back of our terrace house and Dad says *Maybe so, maybe*. We pester him to build a pool on the little lawn, too, and Dad says *Maybe so, maybe*.

And with Dad you never know, because sometimes he comes home with amazing things he's bought that make Mum angry and irritated. We are the first ones in the neighbourhood to have a VCR, and a computer and eventually a CD player. We have an over-sized cream coloured leather sofa and two identical gigantic reclining chairs in the living room, and pretty much nothing else will fit in there because it is actually a really small room. All of the rooms in our little terrace house are small, but Mum and Dad have furnished them as if they are part of a large, detached house.

When I am little my father is the one who barbecues on summer evenings. Mum and our neighbour Gunilla sit on the leather sofa and drink rosé and listen to Agneta Fältskog singing ABBA's 'The Heat is On'. Gunilla works in the make-up department at Domus and I always think she looks pretty in her make-up. She is always tanned and has pink nails. When Gunilla is out of earshot, Dad says bad things about Domus, because Konsum and Blåvitt are the most pathetic things he knows. He votes for the moderates and him and Mum only shop at Ica.

I do not like it when he talks about Gunilla and Domus in that condescending way because I like Gunilla. But Dad uses that voice when he talks about a lot of the neighbours. He puts fillet of beef on the grill and makes Béarnaise sauce and says, 'That bloke thinks he's somebody.'

Gunilla lives with a man named Tommy and sometimes they barbecue together with Mum and Dad. Tommy and Dad drink cocktails from identical crystal glasses like JR in *Dallas* and we get crisps and Fanta. Dad sleeps heavily in the morning and as usual, jumping on the bed does not help; he barely moves. Mum packs juice and crackers in a basket and bikes with us to the city park. When we get home, Dad is still sleeping. Mum gets angry because breakfast is still on the table and the cheese is all sweaty. She goes upstairs and wakes him up and I hear him yell *Stupid bitch! Go to hell!* I take Kajsa and show her the dead bird I found under the apple tree next to the rubbish bins.

Mum has rough hands, which are red and dry from eczema, and dry flakes of skin fall off when she scratches them. Sometimes when she touches my cheek at bedtime it scratches and almost hurts, but I still do not want her to stop. I love my mother's hands, they make me feel calm and safe.

She puts on a pair of yellow rubber gloves when she is doing the dishes, because the dishwater makes her hands sting and bleed. But the plastic gloves are not very good either, because her hands are sweaty and confined, and sometimes she cries because it hurts so much. I go and get the special eczema ointment she buys at the chemist and Mum smiles a little and tries to stop crying.

'Thank you sweetheart!' she says, and I sit next to her and watch while she rubs it on to her sore hands.

Mornings are stressful when we go to daycare. Mum starts work at the hospital at 7 a.m. and she wakes me and Kajsa up at six so we will have enough time. She talks about her mean boss who stands there, watch in hand, waiting at the entrance to the unit. The boss is always quiet and does not say anything when she comes in, he just looks at her and then at his watch.

'If he would only say something,' Mum says as she gets us dressed, 'but he's silent. Do you understand?'

I really do not understand why it is so bad, but Mum gets stressed knowing he is standing there with his watch, waiting, because she dresses us with rough, jerky movements.

Sometimes we fight. My sister is particular about her white plastic headband being in just the right position and her sleeves being exactly the same length. If Mum is just the tiniest bit sloppy, Kajsa loses it and starts screaming at the top of her lungs. I can see the beads of sweat breaking out on Mum's forehead while she is pulling on Kajsa's shirt to get the sleeves the same length. Then it is time to smooth the hair so that each strand ends up in the right place under the white headband.

I stand there staring and I tease Kajsa because she is being so silly until Mum snaps at me angrily, and says to stop teasing and Kajsa sticks her tongue out at me and then we are ready and we head off to daycare. She lifts us up on the bike, Kajsa in front, and me at the back.

We eat breakfast at daycare. It is just me and Kajsa and
Nelly and Emil who eat breakfast there, the other children are
dropped off later. My favourite teacher is Cattis and she and
Mum talk in special adult voices. The tone is warm, confiden-
tial and a bit secretive. I try to hear what they are saying but
they are not talking loudly enough. I carefully creep closer,
until I am standing right behind Mum.

'Just relax, you needn't worry,' Cattis says to Mum. 'It's better if you do the shopping before you pick up the children, then
Sara and Kajsa don't need to go with you to the shop. They're
fine here, you know that!'

I see Mum wipe a tear away and Cattis hands her a tissue
which she uses to blow her nose. I love Cattis because she is
so nice to Mum. She is nice to everyone and always has time
to read thick story books and she never raises her voice. Mum
hugs me goodbye and through the window I watch her bike
away, off to her stupid boss and then we sit down and eat porridge with cinnamon and sugar and milk.

Mum picks us up later in the afternoon. Cattis has gone
home and Lena, a new teacher, greets her. She has only been
working here for two months and she does not know Mum
very well.

'Sorry I'm late,' Mum says, and sets down several heavy
shopping bags on the floor. 'I spoke to Cattis this morning and
said I would be a little late and she said it was fine.'

Lena smiles at Mum. 'Yes, it's fine. I know it's not easy
being a single mother with two young children.'

I see Mum grow quiet, she does not know how to answer.

'I'm not a single parent,' she says after a while, 'my husband
is working a lot at the moment.'

'I see,' Lena says and looks surprised. 'I just thought . . .

well, I've never met your husband so I just assumed you were a single parent.'

'I understand,' Mum says, and starts putting on our coats.

Later that evening, when we are lying in bed and Mum thinks we are asleep, I hear them fighting in the kitchen.

'How do you think it feels?' Mum says. 'First my colleague whom I met in the park on Sunday and now Lena at daycare. Everyone thinks I'm a single parent because you're never here!'

I cannot hear Dad's reply because I put the pillow over my head and imagine I have a nice big brother. His name is Fredrik and he gives me lots of hugs, because he likes me so much. He says that I am the sweetest little sister in the whole world and that he is always going to take care of me. We run along the beach together and go swimming every day during the summer. Fredrik's friends are also there. They like me too and I am allowed to hang out with them as much as I want.

I spend a lot of time thinking about Fredrik. In my mind, I create a family for the two of us with different parents and no younger siblings. In my imaginary family there is just me and Fredrik and our nice Mum and Dad who never fight.

I am lying on my bed at home, thinking about Fredrik when there is a knock at the door. Kajsa comes in and wants to borrow my dolls, and I think about how I would rather have a big brother than a little sister. I shoo her out and say that she is never, ever allowed to come into my room like that! *Damn brat!* I lock the door and go to the playground.

I see Big Johnny on the jungle gym. He lives in one of the terrace houses on the street behind ours and he is a few years older. He is good looking with brown hair and blue eyes, but I do not dare speak to him. Some days he looks angry and sad and sits alone and swings and swings. His parents are *divorced* and now he lives with his mum and he doesn't seem to know anyone in the neighbourhood, but today he sees me walking towards him. He is so good looking, cute actually, and I think that maybe he could be my big brother if he wanted to.

'Hi!' I say, and stop at the base of the jungle gym.

'Hi!' Big Johnny says, and looks down at me.

'Want to play?' I ask.

'Nope,' he says simply, and jumps down from the jungle gym and walks off. I watch him go, his grey hooded jacket and brown boat-shoes disappear between the houses. I remain standing there for a long time, dragging my foot through the sand before I too go home.

Dad has woken up and is sitting alone in the kitchen eating breakfast. He is eating fried eggs and bacon and I can tell from the silence that he and Mum are still quarrelling. I can feel tears burning in my eyes and Dad looks up at me and sees that my neck is covered with red blotches.

'Hey! How's it going?' he says, sounding strangely friendly.

The tears come and I sob. I do not know how to explain the emotions welling up inside me, all the sadness. Maybe that is why I hear myself say something incomprehensible.

'Big Johnny hit me!' I say, and cry even more, frightened by how openly I am lying. I do not know why I said it, or how I dared, but it has been such a strange day, a day filled with sadness.

'He did?' Dad asks, upset, and he hugs me.

'I'll be damned if he's going to go after little girls like that!'

Frightened, I see him get up and grab his coat to leave. I hear him mutter to himself while he is putting on his shoes.

'I'm going to talk some sense into that Big Johnny!'

I remain standing in the kitchen for a little while before I rush upstairs to my room and hide in the closet. I am shaking with excitement, from the wonderful feeling that Dad is going out to defend me. I am shaking with guilt, my lie will soon be discovered and I cry a bit out of fear of Dad's rage and Big Johnny's contempt when he is approached with my false accusation. After a while I hear the front door open and Dad's voice booming as he calls my name. I remain sitting in the closet and do not answer. I hear steps on the stairs, and I suddenly hear his heavy breathing filling the entire room.

'Sara?! Where the hell are you?' He sounds as angry as I feared he would, and for a second, which feels like an eternity, I sit there frozen, without breathing. He finally leaves the room and goes downstairs again. I stay in the closet for a long, long time, and even though I need to pee and my whole stomach aches, it is worth it. A cheap price to pay for enjoying Dad's care and protection.

I wake up at night and try and feel if my heart is beating. I often wake up at night and think I am going to die because my heart beats irregularly.

When I am little, my dad is the only one who is awake at night. He often sits downstairs in the leather sofa drinking spirits and listening to music.

'Dad is a night person,' my sister and I used to say.

I go downstairs and sit on his lap for a while. He listens to my heartbeat and says that it is not anything dangerous. It calms me down and then I can go back to sleep.

One night when I am on my way downstairs I hear him crying. I see him sitting at the kitchen table, leaning over a bowl of popcorn. His tears fall straight down into the popcorn.

I become so frightened I forget about my heart.

ALMOST THERE

Fear of Flying Girl has woken up and is ordering two double whiskys from the kind stewardess mum.

'You think I'm terrible don't you?' she asks me, shamefaced.

'Absolutely not! It's great that you're drinking. I would too if I were afraid of flying. I think I'm going to anyway even though I'm not afraid. Or maybe just because I'm not!' I say happily.

The boyfriend looks at us irritably as we clink glasses. He is reading *Today's Industry* with a serious expression. The economy is the religion of our time. I get the desire to tease him, so I clink glasses again loudly with Fear of Flying Girl, whom I am starting to like more and more. Or feeling more and more sorry for?

Yep, he really looks like a pastor studying his Bible, with his black jacket and white shirt. The stewardess is smiling at us in understanding. I am convinced that she wants us to drink. The whisky warms my stomach and makes me happy. I am listening to Nina Simone, always Nina Simone, my saviour in times of need. Her and the bathtub. And Isadora.

My Isadora Afraid to Fly is still sitting on the plane on her way to Vienna. She looks around and discovers that she recognizes several of the analysts. She has spent many hours with them over the years. Isadora and her husband Bennett have been going to therapy for so long they can barely make the tiniest decision without the analysts holding imaginary deliberations on a cloud above their heads.

> Because the fact was that we'd reached that crucial time in a marriage (five years and the sheets you got as wedding presents have just about worn thin) when it's time to decide whether to buy new sheets, have a baby perhaps, and live with each other's lunacy ever after – or else give up the ghost of the marriage (throw out the sheets) and start playing musical beds all over again.

Their marriage feels tired and the world suddenly seems as though it is filled with interesting and available men as a result. Isadora has a constant, burning longing for sex, dry champagne and wet kisses.

I read this and realize I must try to reconcile myself with the fact that my daydreams are about different things, about loneliness, time and solitude.

Champagne and wet kisses, delightful fucks with strangers – it is like *Dallas*. Like the time I bought a thong just for fun and when we saw my bum in the mirror Johan and I laughed so hard we started crying – the little white string cutting in between my cheeks. It looked so fantastically ridiculous. Like a Sue Ellen, or a Lill-Babs.

The fact is I get just as giggly in the changing room at the gym, where almost all of the women wear thongs. It does not matter how perfectly toned their bums are, I cannot help but visualize small brown stains where the thong cuts in the deepest. Thongs are quite simply nasty and I am anything but a fucking thong-wearing woman right now. Quite the opposite actually: a lonely, cotton underwear-wearing bitter bitch, who will soon be able to sleep for a whole week! Nirvana.

There is a bus waiting at the airport in Tenerife which will take us to the hotel. A female guide tells us about all of the outings we can go on. For example, tomorrow they are organizing a city tour and I am filled with a kind of joy. I am sitting here on my own, in excellent spirits. I look around at the others on the bus. Most of them are older couples, a bit above middle age, one young family and then me. I know that I stand out, and I try to ignore the questioning looks and remember that this is just a guest appearance. Fear of Flying Girl and her boyfriend are sitting a few rows in front of me.

They are sitting quietly, looking out of the bus window and their lack of conversation makes me feel how wonderful it is to be alone. How wonderful it is not to sit there with someone (Johan) and struggle to make conversation, while his silence makes me more and more stressed. Why don't we have anything to talk about? Are we in fact really unhappy, but we just don't know it?

At the hotel, I am again filled with joy. From my balcony I can see the ocean and the surrounding mountains. There is space and time for long, endless thoughts here. And there is a bathtub! I am going to take long, hot baths every night this week!

I go down to the restaurant and order paella and a mineral water. A German couple, a bit over middle aged, is sitting in front of me. She is wearing a light pink outfit, has dyed blonde hair and the kind of mouth that makes you suspect she is an alcoholic, along with a pair of high heels which make her wobble even more. He has glasses and grey hair, looks dissatisfied and a bit intellectual. Are they here to drink or maybe to try and cure her alcoholism? Her speech is slurred and when the waiter comes to take their order her dissatisfied husband tears the menu away from her and orders. It is an aggressive gesture but she ignores it, smiles at him instead and crosses her legs. He does not smile back and after a while she stops smiling and suddenly looks endlessly sad. I cannot stop looking at them and I am so curious. How long has she felt unloved, maybe that is why she started drinking too much?

One October, when several of my friends seemed more than usually unhappy in their relationships, I occupied myself with asking all of my male friends whether they felt loved. All but two said they felt very loved. The answer among my female friends was not as predictable. Doubt was constantly present, even if they felt they were loved most of the time. But the difference between always and most of the time means something. Why did the men seem so much more secure than the women?

This counts for me as well. Regardless of how big the crisis between Johan and myself has been, he has always been more stable, convinced of my love for him as well as his for me, something which has sometimes provoked me excessively.

'Don't you understand that I'm about to leave you!' I screamed once last autumn when everything was so awful. I really was about to leave him. I was daydreaming about living alone with shared custody of Sigge. Still, it was as if it did not really sink in.

'I know that we're good for each other,' he repeated, over and over again.

I have to admit that as much as this exasperated me, it calmed me down. If someone (me) wants to be benevolent they could interpret this steadfastness as an expression of the secure home environment in which Johan grew up. A solid security he left home with, a certainty that he is enough just as he is, that he is loved for who he is. If someone (me) were more conspiratorial it could be seen as an expression of a patriarchal upbringing – an inflated self-righteousness which so many men seem to have picked up along the way.

I realize this is the sort of thing I need to work out. What is blasted structure and what is private angst? How much of an excuse do I have for being a bitter bitch? A pretty strong one if I listen to myself. Experience tells me that. I even keep a list of conspiratorial facts which I sometimes read to remind myself, bitter bitch statistics created from small news items and articles I have read and been upset by over the years.

1. A report from The National Board of Health and Welfare shows that when women become ill the risk of the marriage ending is much greater than when men become ill. The divorce rate for women diagnosed with uterine cancer was twice as high as that of healthy women. For men with prostate cancer on the other hand, the relationship was the opposite. They ran a smaller risk of getting divorced.

2. More women than men donate their organs, but more men than women receive donor organs. This fact was so disheartening that a researcher in social medicine is going to investigate whether this is the

same type of gender discrimination that results in a higher proportion of men receiving costly medical care.

3. A sociological study has shown that more married women suffer from severe mental illness than unmarried ones, but for men it was the opposite: mental illness was greater among unmarried men, while the married men felt just fine. Marriage benefits men and harms women.

4. All injustice: abuse, rape, prostitution, salary discrepancy, a list so comprehensive it can be likened to a form of global apartheid.

The list is endless and that is why it is so hard not to be a bitter bitch even if I didn't want to be one. I think about this a lot: how can I not be a bitter bitch when patriarchal dominance of the world is so incredibly universal, down to the tiniest particle?

Dissatisfied man and his pink alcoholic wife have their food. He takes big bites out of a piece of meat while she pokes at her shrimp salad and drinks even more white wine. I must be staring, because she suddenly raises her glass as if to say cheers to me. I smile and mouth cheers back. The man grunts something in German and continues to eat.

I cannot stop staring at their marital unhappiness. I carefully note it down, letting it grab me for eternity. I never want to lose hold of certain images, certain events, certain knowledge, while some other knowledge will never disappear no matter how much I would like it to. Like this study which found that married women were unhappier than unmarried ones. We know this, and yet hope refuses to die among the millions of hungering women out there, hanging on to a tiny dream that their love is bigger and stronger than damned statistics and bloody culture. But the suspicion is there and it never leaves us alone, the gnawing feeling that I am slowly but surely being drained of my vitality, time and energy.

Or, as the Swedish politician Gudrun Schyman said in what has been called her Taliban speech: women give and men take. I understood exactly what she meant and hearing someone formulate what I had long suspected made me sad. There are certain societal structures, an ideology or religion we might call patriarchy, that makes us expect different things from each other, from love. These structures legitimize men's power and women's powerlessness, making us believe in and live by ancient, rotten gender roles which lead to all of us being deeply unhappy.

But challenging and confronting lovelessness causes pain, and on TV, men like Erik Fichteluis stood, red-faced, and reported on what a disgrace it was that the situation of women in Afghanistan had been compared to that of (spoiled) Swedish women.

And then it did not seem to matter how much Gudrun explained that she wasn't belittling the oppression of women in Afghanistan; she had meant that there is patriarchal oppression in Sweden just as there is in Afghanistan, but that the oppression takes different forms (for example women in Sweden do not wear burkas). Gudrun said that this oppression has its origin in the gender power imbalance, but no one was listening because all we could hear was the red-faced male journalists and commentators screaming about how insulted they were at being called Talibanists.

I am trying to see the humour in it. To a certain extent, these red-faced men on TV are quite funny, but the nonchalance of their message is just a little too irritating. Refusing to admit your own part in oppression is an incredibly smart power strategy, since oppression is made invisible by diminishing it.

It is almost more obvious when it comes to the question of class. I am thinking about all the times I have interviewed people with middle-class backgrounds and when I have asked what class they grew up in, they irritably snap that they do not understand the question, or answer that the idea of class is obsolete, that there are only individual differences. That is what happened with the young fashion expert and newspaper editor I interviewed for a radio programme.

'What kind of neighbourhood did you grow up in?' I asked.

'Örgryte,' the fashion expert replied. One of Göteborg's most affluent areas.

'OK, and how would you describe the area?'

'Well, I don't know. You'll have to call Göteborg's town hall and ask them,' the fashion expert replied.

'But does it mainly have tower blocks, rented accommodation, or houses . . . ?'

'It is mixed,' she said, and looked at me with big, blue eyes. She shook her long, well-cared for blonde hair, and despite the fact that she looked like a Barbie doll I knew she was not stupid, just the opposite. This competent Barbie pretending to be ignorant bothered me, and so I continued asking her about class, until she grew tired and said that if she belonged to a class it was the working class because her parents – mother a doctor and father a shipbroker – worked more than sixty hours a week. When I suggested that doctor and shipbroker were not professions one would consider working class, she said that we are all free to define class as we wish. It was so fantastic in some way, and yet so awful.

The world seems to be divided into two types of people: the ones who think the world is just and those who think it is not. It is mostly men who deny that there is a gender imbalance between men and women. I think it is this denial, more than anything else, that makes me bitter bitchy. I think it has to do with their nonchalance, which creates a feeling of power-lessness and invisibility, as if you have been screaming at the top of your lungs and no one has listened, although you know everyone has heard you. And I am annoyed that it is so effec-tive, perhaps the smartest way of preserving the oppression. The dialogue fades away and you are forced to rewind the tape and start again.

Of course the issue of class is different now compared to a century ago. An uneducated carpet installer may have a higher monthly income than a librarian. The walls that defined class at the beginning of the 1900s have moved. The working class has a different meaning now than it did in 1920. Nevertheless we live in a society where an uneducated nursing assistant lives in a different socio-economic sphere than a blonde fashion expert with a doctor for a mother and shipbroker for a father.

When it comes to the denial of injustice within romantic relationships, there is a never-ending flow of valid reasons to excuse the power imbalance. Along with humiliation and invisibility you have the additional difficulty of defining love. I think a lot about love being what love does; that if we started seeing love more as an action than as an emotion then responsibility and obligations would automatically follow. If we stopped viewing love as just an emotion, it would be easier to counter the argument that love can take different forms for different individuals. We might avoid the romanticized Hollywood images that obscure problems in a relationship, the idea that love becomes dull without romance, roses and champagne. Stories I have read a thousand times which suggest that what I am missing can be boiled down to a bouquet of cut flowers. I can easily live without roses and champagne, but I cannot put up with inequality; it should not exist in a relationship in which two people claim to love each other. Perhaps we tell ourselves that love means different things to different people, because if we try to define love we will be forced to see what we are missing?

What I hate most about being a bitter bitch is the feeling of pettiness which is slowly taking hold, an evil cycle of nitpicking which is difficult to stop. I let the small things become big ones. I do not want to be a petty, small-minded person, but generosity is a luxury which can only exist when you feel good and are treated justly and affectionately.

The more I think about it, the clearer it becomes: love, the greatest thing of all, has been kidnapped by patriarchy, capitalism and Hollywood, and transformed into something significantly smaller and phonier. Marriage has been kidnapped in the same way. Instead of being a pure manifestation of love it has become something associated with royalty, Carl Bildt and other non-Socialist groups as well as conventions which get etiquette expert Magdalena Ribbing cheering from her flat on Öfvre Östermalm. We no longer see that the institute of marriage obscures pure love, the greatest of all. The fact that I was forced to joke about my marriage after only a month is not so strange after all; nor is it strange, that because of my ideal of equality, I did not really want to be married. I just wanted to have a lovefest.

It is not strange that I sit here in Tenerife, unable to stop my bitter cunt thoughts, my pitch-black observations. I cannot turn a blind eye to the word any longer, and maybe this is what makes me bitter? I know too much. I know that women often blossom when the initial pain of the divorce has settled, while men suddenly discover how lonely they are. They realize what a bad relationship they have with their children, how few friends they have, since their wives were the ones who took care of the children and the friends and the family while the men worked and made their careers. Men also pay a price for their superiority. A woman with tired legs and a migraine stands behind every successful man. And a divorce is behind every successful woman.

They are getting up now and leaving, the alcoholic woman and her dissatisfied husband. He doesn't look at her, instead he walks with determined steps towards the exit and she wobbles after him on her high heels. She tries to keep up while ignoring his angry rejection of her. Perhaps they sometimes lie awake at night and wonder why they got married in the first place. Everything you thought would happen when you get married has not and suddenly thirty years have passed and you realize you have become a bit tipsy and unhappy and your husband is ashamed of you and always walks a few feet ahead. You take a one week holiday to Tenerife and put on a cock-coloured outfit and high-heeled pumps, and it does not help, even though you try and coordinate it with pink lipstick and perfume. You wobble anyway.

I get up too and go and lie down on one of the sun loungers around the pool, thinking to myself that there must be something terribly wrong; being this tired should not be allowed.

I fall into a deep sleep and dream that I am in New York. I am travelling and I am happy and everything is exciting but further down the street I hear a choir of women's voices. At first I think they are singing but when I get closer I can hear that they are screaming. They are angry about something but I cannot make out the words and a man who looks like Arnold Schwarzenegger has stood up on a bench to try and calm them down. When I get closer I see that it *is* Arnold Schwarzenegger and I feel a bit sorry for him, even though I suspect the women have a right to be upset. His hair is so grey and his eyes look so tired and sad. Suddenly he pulls off his shirt and reveals his muscular, oiled torso. The screaming women fall silent for a moment, surprised, and Arnold happily takes the opportunity to flex his arm muscles and suck in his stomach. A real bodybuilder. When the women realize he has started posing instead of answering them they become even angrier. Large tears start to roll down Arnold's wounded cheeks. He still does not understand what he has done wrong. Poor devil, I must help him, but the screams drown out everything else and I am forced to lean up close so he will be able to hear me.

'Men also pay a price for their superiority! You have to pay a high price for your power. Do you understand?'

He looks at me, confused and tries to answer, but the women scream so loudly I cannot hear what he is saying.

The sound of arguing children in the pool wakes me. Their mother is yelling at them to get out of the water, NOW! There is no father. There are never any fathers screaming hysterically at their children out of exhaustion. They are probably sitting in the bar, drinking beer and chatting.

I am thinking about my dream, that is it is only a fragile comfort that men also pay a price for their superiority. The oppression of women costs far more. There are lots of reasons for my bitter bitch transformation and it has been going on my whole life, but nothing has been as painful, as terribly bitter bitch making, as that of becoming a mother. Of all myths it is probably the holiest, that of becoming a mother, which is the most untrue, the most painful.

A NEW WAY OF MEASURING TIME
(2002)

I am pregnant and constantly worried about having a miscarriage. I dream about bloody clumps running down, out of my body, and I wake up sweaty and sad. I want this child so much!

Johan tries to calm me down and feels my breasts. 'They've changed. They weren't this big before.'

But it does not help. I read books which outline the symptoms of pregnancy and conclude that I do not have a single one. I do not feel sick, I am not tired, I have not lost my sex drive. I feel normal, completely entirely bloody abnormally normal.

And I am not looking forward to childbirth. My friends who have had children talk about childbirth as though it is the most fantastic thing they have ever experienced. I listen with a wrinkled brow and a suspicious look.

'It's the greatest kick! Like running a marathon!' Charlotte says enthusiastically.

But I would never, ever run a marathon voluntarily, I think to myself. I do not have any desire to manage that kind of physical achievement. We rent a house on Gotland during the summer with some friends. We bike several kilometres to different beaches each day and I am strong and sunburned. I study my body in the mirror in our bedroom. Maybe my stomach has started growing just a little? I stop dreaming about bloody, slimy clumps and when we get back to Stockholm I start to believe that maybe there will be a baby after all.

During the ultrasound we see our baby clench its fist. A victory sign, the sign of a fighter. A sign to us that everything is going to be fine. We start daring to joke about names and we start calling the baby Sue Ellen.

One morning when I get up to use the bathroom I see that everything is red. At first I do not understand, I wipe myself and I see how the paper turns red from the blood. Bloody urine. It is almost orange.

Sue Ellen has been in my stomach for twenty-two weeks, it is too late for a damn miscarriage! I cannot have a miscarriage now, not when I have just started relaxing! We call the hospital and they tell us to come in to the Maternity Ward to check things out. I am crying and Johan is quiet and resolute. Maybe the taxi driver cannot see that I am crying in the back seat, because when he drops us off he says: 'Good luck!'

Johan mumbles 'Thanks!' and pays.

I am examined and when I hear our baby's heartbeat I stop crying. Sue Ellen is OK! The doctor slides the ultrasound device across my belly and sees that the placenta is lying too far down, over the cervix.

'That's probably why you had some bleeding,' he says, as he washes his hands.

We stay in for two days for observation and another doctor tells us that we should prepare for having a planned Caesarean. She says it with regret and looks at us questioningly when we grin at each other, elated that we do not have to worry about childbirth!

After a few days at the hospital we go home. We have been warned that there could be more bleeding during the remainder of the pregnancy. Every time it happens we must go to the hospital. I receive strict orders to take it easy from now on. No heavy grocery bags, no biking, and as much rest as possible. Yes, yes, yes, I say, relieved that my baby is OK. It is the only thing that matters.

We have only been home for a few hours when the doorbell rings. It is a delivery man with a marzipan cake. It says *Sue Ellen* in chocolate letters across the middle. Johan's sister and her boyfriend have sent it. We stand across from each other at the kitchen table and look at the ornate handwriting. The chocolate name, our baby! Johan's eyes fill with tears for the first time and we cry and eat cake the rest of the night, sitting really, really close.

My midwife wants me to go on sick leave but I refuse. I am afraid of the silence, the rest, the thoughts, afraid of stopping, of not having a job, an identity. I am afraid of becoming one of those – a pregnant woman on sick leave. A mother lizard. I tell her that work is fine and I do not mention the heavy tape recorder I have to lug with me to every interview. I do not tell her anything about the bustle, about the stress, about my need for achievement. How is she to know that my strength is my standard, that I despise all signs of weakness?

I am working more than ever before. I have a full-time substitute position and I am also working on a documentary. People around me sigh and do not know that I interpret this as proof of my strength. Pretending to be strong makes me feel good. I almost get used to the bleeding, which comes now and again. I get used to going to the hospital every time it happens, being examined, staying overnight on a hard delivery bed and going to work the next morning. Straight from the Maternity Ward. I feel strong and able and, strangely enough, less and less afraid the more I challenge fate.

This feeling continues until three days before the planned Caesarean. The night before I become genuinely terrified. It creeps up on me, that suspicion of the chaos, the ultimate defeat, a complete breakdown . . .

Me.

Nina Simone's 'I Shall Be Released' is playing as Sigge is brought into the world.

In the theatre room, ten fantastic women work on sewing me back together. I am lying on the table crying and I love all ten of them. Worn out, underpaid and yet the whole time they are friendly and filled with patience, comfort and warmth. I am so grateful!

Johan gets to go with the midwife to the room next door where they wash Sigge before they come back and put him on my chest. We have the most wonderful little bundle of joy in the world! He does not want to open his eyes, instead he just lies quietly and I stroke his cheek, hands, feet and back. I love him deeply and earnestly.

The Maternity Ward is wonderful and I do not want to go home. We have our own room where we live in a safe bubble with full support, full service. I do not sleep at all at night, completely absorbed in lying and watching Sigge, but the food is served regularly and there is fresh bread for breakfast. I do not have to think about anything practical, we can focus all of our energy, all of our emotions, unhindered on Sigge and each other. The only thing that does not really work is the breastfeeding. My breasts are swollen with milk which just runs and runs, but Sigge has a hard time latching on. Finally the midwife helps us with a nipple shield which you put on the breast and then he is able to suck a little bit.

After four days we are forced to leave the safety bubble for home. We are in a daze and I cry and cry. I think it is from happiness, or it is exhaustion?

When we have been home for two days a set designer comes over, one Johan is going to work with on his next production. It is Johan's first job since he finished his stage management course at the University College of Film, Radio, Television and Theatre, and he is looking forward to it with expectation and anxiety. It means a lot to him. The set designer and Johan lock themselves in the study. I sit in the living room trying to breastfeed Sigge and it doesn't go very well. My breasts are hard and swollen and small angry streams of milk are leaking out, wetting my shirt. They sting and burn and want to be emptied, but Sigge roars with fury every time I put him to my breast. I try and brace myself, I try to keep his crying from cutting deep into my insides. I try and sound calm, soft when I say, 'There you go sweetheart . . . there you go . . . please try sweetie . . .'

I stroke his head and back, I stroke his feet. I let his angry hand cling desperately to my index finger. His little body is tense like a bow and he is shaking with rage. His cries make me sweat, it runs from my forehead, down into my eyes, under my arms, over my stomach and down my thighs. I panic. I panic because I cannot defend myself against his cries any longer. I panic because it will bother the set designer and Johan and they will wonder why he is crying so much, because I am sitting here trying to be considerate of them when it should be

the other way around. What the hell is that set designer doing
here anyway? I need Johan here now, next to me on the sofa.
I realize that I am alone. Am I supposed to solve this problem
alone? I cannot get Sigge to take the breast although he is hungry. I start to panic because this baby has taken possession of
me.

I put Sigge against my shoulder and carry him around the
room. He grows quiet and I feel his little body relax. I put on
Nina Simone and dance with him and let the tears come. I sob
quietly so that Johan and the set designer will not hear. I long
for the Maternity Ward, for the red button you could push as
soon as you needed help. A push of the button and the friendly
midwife women with soothing words and comforting hands
would come. I was not alone at the Maternity Ward.

The next day a scriptwriter with whom Johan has upcoming
projects stops by. They lock themselves in the study and hold
a meeting. We have been home for four days and I have started
to shiver. I walk around in thick socks and a jumper and I turn
up the heating. The rooftops outside are silver with November
frost and I wonder if I will ever be brave enough to go outside
again? What do you do when your child starts screaming and
you long to leave home?

My life has changed completely. My body has gone through
a war and is now occupied by a foreign power. The one I saw
as my ally has turned out to be a traitor. A betrayer, completely absorbed in other things, other meetings. And I try to
understand.

I stare into Sigge's eyes and try and get to know my little
occupying power. I appease him by using a nipple shield, and
I get him to eat a little bit. He falls asleep full, and I take the

opportunity to make some sandwiches that I gobble down for lunch, and then I watch TV with Sigge in my arms. I am a bit worried because Johan will be going to a meeting in Skellefteå tomorrow. It is at the provincial theatre where his production will take place in a few months, and I am worried about being alone with Sigge for a whole day. It has only been four days since we came home from the hospital and everything is new and overwhelming. I am worried about the breastfeeding not working. I am worried because I have not slept in six days. I am worried that the incision from the Caesarean is hurting.

I am worried because I notice that Johan's thoughts are elsewhere.

I wake up at six in the morning because one of my breasts is rock hard and it hurts. Breast engorgement. I stumble to the bathroom in the November morning darkness. I have read that you should massage and warm the breast when you get breast engorgement, so I aim the hair dryer at my breast. The noise wakes Johan, and when he comes into the bathroom everything falls apart and I sob, 'Johan please don't go! I'm in pain and I don't want to be alone today!' Johan looks desperate. 'But I have to go. The whole theatre company is waiting for me.' The milk is running, snot is dripping, tears are falling. I am a clump of slime which will soon drip down the drain and I scream in order to overpower the hair dryer, 'To hell with your stupid theatre!'

But Johan's flight leaves at seven, and fifteen minutes later he disappears out through the door. I remain sitting in the bathroom on the toilet with the hair dryer, crying and crying. I finally calm myself down and take two paracetamol and crawl into bed next to Sigge's warm little body. I wake up two hours later, drenched in sweat, with a fever and my tender, tennis-ball breast. I try and nurse Sigge with my healthy breast and then he gets to lie on a blanket on the kitchen floor while I try to eat some breakfast, I do not dare think about the fact that Johan left. That he walked out the door even though I asked him to stay. I brush against the unthinkable but let it stay there, like a well-hidden ulcer.

I put the oven on high and sit down in front of it naked in the hope that the heat will help, but it does not. The fever just keeps rising and I am shivering all over. I take more paracetamol and get into bed beneath a mountain of blankets with Sigge and I only get up when I am forced to change his nappy.

Finally Johan comes home late at night, filled with guilt and worry.

'I've been thinking about you all day,' he says, with tears in his eyes.

It does not help me a damn bit that you have been thinking about us all day, I think to myself. But I do not say anything. I am so exhausted and in so much pain, I do not have the energy to be angry.

When the breast engorgement has not passed after three days and the thermometer reads 41°C, we rush to the hospital. I am given antibiotics and sent home with some friendly nursing tips. Apparently stopping the breastfeeding is not an option. The next day I already feel much better, almost no temperature. But the thermometer reads 39°C, so it is only the difference between 41°C and 39°C which makes me feel better. The next day the temperature rises and then we are off to the emergency room again. This time I am admitted.

We get our own room so that Johan and Sigge can stay. My fever is now at 40°C and I am either drenched in sweat or freezing. In the afternoon, two women from the hospital breastfeeding office come down. They want to see if I can nurse Sigge without the nipple shield. I am sitting there in an ugly hospital chair, sweating from the fever and Sigge is crying because he cannot nurse without the nipple shield. One of the women grabs and pulls at my nipple and tries to position it correctly in Sigge's mouth. It hurts, but my breasts are no longer my own. They just happen to be attached to my body, producing milk. After ten long minutes, where I have tried to get a hysterical Sigge to nurse, while the women stand and watch, I ask if I can stop.

'Well, I suppose we can stop for now,' one of them says. She has a small gold cross around her neck and small white pearl earrings. I suddenly remember reading somewhere that there are many liberals in health care. They never start a revolution, often believe in God and pray to him instead of striking for better working conditions. Maybe it is the fever or because they are just standing there, staring at me, or maybe it is because I am soaked in sweat, but I suddenly become furious at the nursing lady with the gold cross.

'I'm actually thinking about stopping the breastfeeding since it's not working. I've heard about some pills you can take which stop lactation. Wouldn't that make the breast engorgement go away?' I say.

The nursing ladies become upset.

'Those pills are very dangerous, they can make you psychotic,' says one of them.

'You shouldn't give up so easily. You can always count on breastfeeding being difficult for the first few months,' says the one with the gold cross and the pearl earrings.

'I'm not going to make it through the month and I'll probably become psychotic anyway from constant pain and fever. Do you get that?!' I scream.

The nursing ladies look at each other knowingly and then at me. They probably think I am crazy and hysterical. And I am.

'Well, everything will be fine, you'll see,' says the golden cross lady.

'Unfortunately we have to go now but you can contact us again if you need any nursing help.'

They leave and I cry and sweat and my breasts are leaking milk which Sigge cannot get inside him.

I put the nipple shield on again and try my best to nurse Sigge. Two days later we are allowed to go home. Johan and I have decided to start supplementing the second-rate breast-feeding with formula. It works and our concern about Sigge not getting enough food disappears now that we can see exactly how much he is eating. We go for a walk for the first time with Sigge in the buggy. Johan takes a picture of me when I am standing next to the sea. I am leaning on the buggy and I look tired.

But it is a difficult time in every sense of the word, and the next day my healthy breast really starts hurting. It is slowly transformed into a hard tennis ball and the temperature returns. The hospital says we have to come in again imme-diately, and I cry. I do not want to go to the hospital again! I am lying on our bed under several layers of thick blankets, shaking from the fever. Johan is sitting on the edge of the bed.

'Wouldn't it be better for Sigge's sake if he and I stay home so that you can rest and get better?' He strokes my hair.

It takes a moment before I understand that Johan does not want to come with me to the hospital. I do not want to go there either, but I have to, and the thought of having to be away from Sigge for a whole night fills me with a raging fear. It feels physically impossible. I cannot believe he is serious. He cannot be serious!

Johan changes his mind and says that of course they can come with me, but he does not want to stay overnight. He and Sigge can come and visit during the day but go home at night. I try to explain that I must have Sigge with me. His warm little body, his small gasping breaths which calm me down. But Johan does not understand what I am thinking and says that if he was sick, he wouldn't want me and Sigge to stay with him. What kind of an argument is that, since I am the one who is sick and want him and Sigge to stay with me? I am suddenly overwhelmed by hate. I become ice cold.

'Do you understand that I'm never, ever going to be able to forgive you for this?'

Johan looks dejected and goes and calls a taxi.

The hospital is full and we are shown to a room with several beds. I look at Johan and hate him because he looks so content.

'You see I can't stay now?' he says in a regretful tone. I look at the woman in the white coat next to us. She does not make eye contact with me, instead she is looking down at her pager which she fingers nervously.

'Unfortunately we're short on single rooms tonight. Your husband and your baby won't be able to stay here overnight,' she says quietly.

Does she suspect my desperation? Does she notice my sweat? Does she know that a high temperature makes you boundless and crazy?

The tears start coming again. I am getting used to it, the

sensation of my red, puffy face which never has time to dry
from the tears and the snot. A moan grows inside me, starting
in my stomach, and moves up through my throat. I am crying
in a way I never have before, loud and guttural. I sound like a
wounded animal, it sounds horrid and I know it is embarrass-
ing for those in the normal world to which I no longer belong. I
hear the nurse leave the room and Johan tries to sit next to me
on the bed. I push him away and I take Sigge and crawl under
the covers with him next to me. I stroke his little head, look at
his beautiful, sleeping face. My beloved child, the most beautiful little baby, who creates a loving ache of a special kind in
my entire chest.

I do not know how long we lie like this. Johan is sitting
quietly in the light pink hospital chair, looking out of the
window. There is a painting on the wall above him. A water-
colour of a meadow with innocent flowers. There is a sunset
in the background which colours everything pink. My sense
of humour disappeared a long time ago and I think about how
much I hate the colour pink. The ugliest colour, disgusting in
all ways and yet so common.

After a while I notice that Johan is starting to get his things
together. He puts on his coat and gets ready to go. He stands
next to my bed and tries to look me in the eyes, but I refuse to
look at him. Suddenly the door opens and the woman with the
white coat comes in. She heads straight for my bed and looks
happy.

'We found a room for you!' she says proudly. 'So the whole
little family can stay!'

Johan wrinkles his eyebrows but does not let go of the bag
he is holding tightly in his hand.

'When you became so upset we felt sorry for you and well,

now you can stay,' she says happily, and looks at Johan. He looks back at her stiffly and then at me.

'But . . . I really think it's best for all of us if Sigge and I go home.'

Now Johan is the one who refuses to look me in the eye. I can see he is ashamed and angry and I can hear him struggling to sound pleasant.

'It's starting to get late now so you need to sleep Sara, and we'll come tomorrow and visit.'

I look at his face, turned away, and realize that I do not have the energy to fight any more. The paracetamol has stopped working and I can feel my temperature rising again. A familiar chill spreads through my body and I start to shake. I do not say anything and I know that my silence makes him nervous.

'OK, well, you do as you please,' says the woman in the white coat, confused, and she leaves us alone.

Johan has picked up Sigge and started putting on his snow-suit, and I continue to avoid eye contact with him. Maybe this is what it is like when you start becoming apathetic, I think to myself.

But when I see Sigge leave the room in the car seat Johan is carrying, I come to life. Something snaps and I become furious and run after them. In my half-psychotic feverish world I see a monster kidnap my child and I have to save him. But the incision makes me double over and I fall in a heap on the floor. I remain lying there, watching the walls of the room sway. I think I have become crazy for real now. I sob and sniffle because my child is lost, I am lost. The woman in the white coat comes in; she must having been waiting outside. She helps me into bed and tucks me in.

'There now,' she says in a kind voice, while she strokes my hair. But I cannot stop crying.

'I've had a baby!' I sob. 'And he's so beautiful. The most beautiful little thing!'

'Of course he is!' says the kind nurse.

'But I don't want to die now. I want him close to me!'

'Now now, you're not going to die. We'll make sure of that.'

She sits for a long time and strokes my hair. It calms me down and after a while I stop crying.

The hospital bed is hard and narrow and I lie awake the whole night, staring at the ceiling. I think horrible thoughts about never seeing Sigge again. He is going to die tonight, of SIDS. The taxi is in an accident. I cannot stop, the images just keep coming, one after the other, each one is worse.

Over the next five days they try six different kinds of antibiotics which I am given through an IV, but nothing helps. The fever never drops below 39°C.

I only remember fragments of these days. Johan and Sigge come in the afternoons. Me crying when I get to have Sigge next to me in bed. Me crying when they leave at the end of the afternoon. The nights where I cannot sleep. My death-like anxiety when I notice that even the doctors are starting to get worried. No one can say anything, and then there is this fever which is making me crazy. I tell Johan it is just typical that I would die now when I have finally had Sigge. He tries to comfort me but I can tell that he is worried, too.

Finally I get the anti-breastfeeding pills I have asked for. The milk slowly goes away but my breasts are still hard and sore. They discover that I have contracted a resistant hospital bacteria on top of my mastitis, which is why the antibiotics haven't been helping. I cannot help thinking that I got it from the nursing ladies when they were pinching at my nipples. We can even laugh about that, Johan and I.

I am not able to deal with the extent of his betrayal. I put it away and hide it well and it will take ten months before I can even use the word betrayal. During this period I do not tell anyone what I have experienced. Instead I use Johan's version. I say that Johan and Sigge could not stay at the hospital because it was so difficult for them to be there, that it was better for both Sigge and me if they slept at home.

After a week I am allowed to come home, and it is a blessing to be free from the fever. Sigge drinks formula from a bottle and Johan and I can share the feeding times. The invasion is over and my love for my bundle of joy can blossom free of illness, fever sweats and leaking breast-milk. I can even catch up on some sleep because we are splitting the night-time feeds. The bottle and the formula are my liberators and I set about conquering life again, ecstatically. Johan, on the other hand, is stressed. While I have been sick he has been forced to postpone all of his meetings and now he has to make up for it.

I feel an unspoken guilt about Johan not being able to work as planned. Maybe I am imagining it, but the feeling is there and I do not object when he starts working as soon as we have come home. It was only later that I thought how strange it was that we did not take a break then, take some time to recover.

The days pass and my illness has become something we tremble at together, almost out of pleasure. We laugh so hard we cry when we find out that my old daycare teacher, Cattis, asked a church congregation in our hometown of Västerås to hold an intercession for us. They prayed that the sick mother would be reunited with her newborn baby, that the little family would be able to come home again.

It is as if all of this is about someone else, an acquaintance I have heard of but do not know that well. I refuse to know. The anxiety and worry have worn me out. I want to be happy again, I also want to know what it feels like to be a happy new mother. There is not any time for sorrow either, Johan is working and I am alone with Sigge during the day. I rush through the days, making the hours go by as quickly as possible. During this time I get to hear how I am beaming. Oh how I am beaming.

In the beginning insomnia can have a manic effect, and I am dizzy with insomnia. It feels good, a bit like being drunk. It is only after a while that the insomnia makes you tired and insane. I get really tired when Johan runs off to Skellefteå to start the rehearsals for his production. For ten weeks straight, Johan is gone from Monday to Friday.

The first week goes really well. On Friday night I am waiting at home with red wine, pizza and lots of longing. We only clash a little when I notice that Johan is absent and tired. He has a hard time talking, just sits there on the sofa, quiet and absorbed in his thoughts about his art. We fall asleep soundly, but then I am woken by Sigge. Johan sleeps on. Like many men he has the fantastic ability to sleep soundly even if the world is coming to an end around him. Or like now, when our baby is whimpering and sleeping fitfully and needs to be carried around for a while in order to fall properly asleep again.

The second week is not so good. I get by but I have a sour taste in my mouth the whole time. An irritation slowly grows inside me, taking on such large proportions that it cannot be ignored.

On Friday night we fight about the fact that I need the weekends, especially the nights, in order to rest. Johan does not think that is a given, because he too is tired after working for an entire week.

I find this difficult to comprehend, since he gets to sleep uninterrupted five nights a week. Again I have a horrible foreboding, a feeling that I do not really know him, this man with whom I have been living for seven years.

Everything is surreal and the floor is moving. I do not know how I am going to get him to understand what it means to be alone with a three-month-old baby around the clock. It is something you cannot understand if you have not experienced it. My overwrought state finally takes the upper hand and my screams drown out Johan's, and he gives in, perhaps because he senses how close I am to the edge? The weekend nights are mine, a small possibility of survival to which I cling.

The days are filled with walks, grocery shopping, long café visits with friends, baby swimming, baby movies, museum visits, clothes shopping. There is lots to do every day, a packed schedule I tend carefully. I am terrified of the quiet, lonely evenings when the thoughts overpower me. Sigge just sleeps in his buggy and when he is awake he is happy. He views the world with curiosity and only cries when he is hungry. My beloved baby, my best friend and my indomitable occupying power.

At the Child Health Centre I get to fill in a form. The health visitor Monika explains that it is a means of detecting the ones who are not feeling well and offering them some help. The questions are about how I experience the every day. Am I anxious? Is it hard to get out and come up with things to do? I am terrified that she is going to find out how unhappy I am, afraid that something is going to break, permanently. I check

all of the boxes indicating that I am feeling great, that I am getting enough sleep, that I am finding things to do every day, that
there really are not any problems in my new life as a mother
at all . . .

Monika looks surprised at my answers.

'OK . . . this looks good. Most people find it a bit difficult in
the beginning before they establish a routine . . .'

I explain that I struggled when I was sick and so compared
to that everything is fantastic. Monika is quiet for a long time,
maybe she sees through me. She cannot possibly know that
my problem is not the lack of things to do, quite the opposite,
that I never stop to rest.

'Of course, the nights are a bit difficult,' I say, in order to
sound a bit more convincing.

'Yes, it's like that for everyone,' Monika says, and I can see
her decide to swallow my over-confidence.

'Try to sleep a bit during the day, when Sigge does,' she tells
me, and I think that I would never be able to or have time, that
is how full my days are.

In the evenings I cry with exhaustion. Sigge lies next to
me in bed and looks seriously into my eyes. He looks sad and
tired too from all of our running around, the hysterical tempo
I maintain each day. I stroke his head and we fall asleep several
hours later.

Johan calls and we do not have anything to say to each other.
He is in the middle of rehearsals and is anxious that the actors
are not taking him seriously, that it will turn out badly, that
he is not good enough. I am quiet and wonder how we will ever
connect again.

Every day I hate him a little bit more. I hate his absence,
which makes me feel lonely and abandoned, feelings that take

me far, far away to an early childhood of which I have no conscious memory. I am shrinking.

Early one Saturday morning, when Johan gets up to change Sigge's nappy, I suddenly hear a thud. There is silence for a few seconds and then I hear a panic filled scream from Sigge. I rush out of bed and see Johan rocking Sigge in his arms.

'He fell from the changing table,' Johan says, shocked. 'I only turned away for a second.' He looks helpless and ashamed but none of this breaks through my iciness.

'Give me Sigge!' I say coldly.

'I want to comfort him,' Johan says with tears in his eyes.

'You can't comfort him. Give me Sigge!' I say again and take Sigge from him.

Sigge soon stops crying and I sit with him in my arms and watch him become his usual self again. I sit there and hate and hate. I curse the fact that Johan is always tired in the morning, curse him because he has not been home and noticed that Sigge can roll over now, curse his entire existence.

We are quiet the whole way to the hospital. We get our own room and a doctor who asks a thousand suspicious questions and makes Johan feel even guiltier. Johan explains that he has been gone a lot and did not know that Sigge had started rolling over. I do not say anything to help him, I just sit there and hate and stare meanly. We stay a few hours for observation and when the doctor leaves the room Johan starts crying. A quiet, tense crying which makes his shoulders shake. For a brief moment I have the impulse to drop everything and just comfort him, cry with him, make up and reach out to him and share our unhappiness, but the knot inside me from the insomnia, the loneliness and the anxiety is too hard. As if all of the longing and abandonment of my childhood, all the disappointment I have ever experienced, wells up and freezes my love for Johan.

And the dryer which is our life continues to toss us around and around for another eight weeks. I call the family guidance office and make an appointment. The woman I talk to does not understand what I mean at first.

'But why was your husband gone for ten weeks?'

Once again I sound like Johan, and I explain that he had contracted to do a job. She sounds uncertain when she asks if she has understood me correctly: our son is only three months old. When I reply that that is correct she grows quiet for some time. Maybe she is taking notes, but the faint uncertainty clings to me. I need confirmation that I am allowed to feel the way I do. I keep thinking that there are millions and millions of women who have been far more betrayed by their husbands, left alone with children without the merest excuse.

The weight of history should not be underrated. I know that a lot of people would snort at my problems. It still makes me doubt my equilibrium. Am I allowed to use a word like betrayal? Johan does not think so. He thinks we were victims of unfortunate circumstances, a difficult situation over which we had no control. But I cannot help thinking that so much could have been different, despite the unfortunate circumstances.

We have an appointment for Thursday morning. Our friends Patrik and Jens are babysitting and they are going to take Sigge for a walk in his baby carriage in the park outside for an hour. The therapists are a middle-aged pair, a team. Their names are Maggan and Mats, and Johan and I giggle nervously at their professional pleasantry. They have woven art on the wall, a rug representing rugged, staring faces. Maggan tells a long story about the origin of the hanging; it was made by a friend of hers and symbolizes the necessary chaos of life. We listen and nod politely.

'Well,' says Mats, 'Sara, why don't you tell us why you wanted to meet with us?'

'We've ended up in a crisis because Johan's been gone so much and has been working constantly since the birth of our first child. It has been much more difficult than I expected, and I've felt abandoned and unloved and I feel like Johan doesn't understand how difficult it has been.'

Maggan and Mats nod and look at Johan.

'I also think it's unfortunate that I was away so much after Sigge was born, but I don't think I had a choice. It was a job I had signed on for and I had to do it.'

Maggan and Mats nod again.

At first we talk carefully and thoughtfully. A calm tennis match begins, as the opponents get a feel for each other, but the tempo slowly changes, encouraged as we are by Maggan and Mats' silence and understanding nods. Soon we are in the middle of a raging storm, the words rush out and we both have flushed complexions from the emotions bursting forth in the room with the woven rug. Finally we grow quiet and Maggan and Mats look at us, expressionless. I wonder if that is something you have to learn as a therapist, not to show how you really feel? Mats runs his palm over his right leg, as if calming it down. Maggan wets her lips and looks at me.

'What I hear when I listen to you is that you constantly come back to the word "equality". It seems to be an important word for both of you, a kind of mantra? She raises her well-plucked eyebrows in order to underline her question.

'Yes,' I reply.

'Yes,' says Johan.

Maggan smiles and looks at Mats who stops running his hand over his trouser leg and smiles back at Maggan. A secret understanding.

'This is something we often hear from couples. You aren't alone in having problems with this so-called "equality",' says Mats. 'And Maggan and I always say the same thing, that trying to attain equality in a romantic relationship is something you can forget about! You must accept that equality is an impossible goal in any relationship. Achieving equality is impossible!'

Johan looks at me and I look at Mats and then at Maggan, trying to understand what he has just said. I do not know what to say and before I have time to think of something, Maggan continues.

'Then this about Johan having to work so much, well, that's the way it has been since the stone age. Men have always had the responsibility of hunting and bringing home the food.' She grins at both of us.

I smile back, a smile which is transformed into a hysterical giggle. I do not dare look at Johan because I know we are going to start laughing if we make eye contact. I can see out of the corner of my eye that Johan is struggling to look straight ahead at the woven hanging. He is sitting unnaturally upright and is holding his head still, but his shoulders are shaking uncontrollably with suppressed laughter.

'And women have always been at home in the cave, minding the children while the men are out hunting. So if I give up my career and become a housewife and drop all of these stupid demands for equality, then we won't argue any more! That's great! Thanks, you've just solved our entire problem. I don't understand why we did not come up with it ourselves!' I say, and grin at Maggan and Mats. Surprised, they look at Johan, who is staring at a spot on the floor.

'Look, this isn't something we're just saying. Many research-ers make this point at seminars,' Mats says, and does not sound quite so professional now.

'You'll have to excuse us,' says Johan. 'But as we've just explained to you, our entire conflict is about how we can live equally. So when you say that there's no point in striving for equality it's the same as telling us to give up.'

'What we mean is that equality can take many forms. If Sara is better at cooking, then it's better if Sara does it. And Johan might be better at changing the tyres on the car?' Maggan says in a professional tone.

'We don't have a car,' says Johan.

'OK. But maybe you're the one who puts up shelves? What I mean is that it isn't always possible to split all tasks equally. Some things feel more natural to you, Sara, and others more natural to Johan?' Maggan says irritably.

I have stopped smiling and started staring at Maggan with cold eyes.

'And what I mean is that I've never experienced a more unnatural situation than being left at home alone with a three-month-old baby for ten weeks. It's probably the most perverted thing a new mother can experience!' I say in a shrill tone. 'How dare you sit here and tell unhappy couples that they shouldn't struggle for equality?' I scream at Maggan and Mats, who are staring back at me with furrowed brows.

I get up and start putting on my coat. Johan does the same and Maggan's voice sounds surly now.

'I assume you don't want to make a new appointment then?'

'NO THANK YOU!' Johan and I say in unison, and leave

the room with the woven wall-hanging as quickly as we can. Away, away from Maggan and Mats and the stone age and the cave people. We walk down the steps towards the park where Patrik and Jens are waiting with Sigge in the buggy. Towards the present and the future. Johan takes my hand in his and we look at each other in perfect understanding and we start laughing. It is a good feeling. I kiss Johan's hand and he stops and pulls me towards him.

'Thanks for being so damned wonderful!' he says and looks me in the eye.

'Thank you for being so damned wonderful!' I say and kiss him.

Our devotion to each other, the laughter which is suddenly there again, keeps us warm for about three days. Then it is Monday and Johan disappears and leaves us alone for yet another week. The emptiness is unbearable. The short moment of closeness we had makes me burn with longing, makes me remember what it felt like before. I had forgotten.

During the week my insomnia and loneliness transform my longing into a rage which makes me red-eyed. When Johan comes home on Friday night I do not have anything to give him and he is tired and distant. I go to bed early and he stays up late watching football. The silence is almost worse than the fighting, but the worst thing of all is the total lack of humour. The sulky, irritating, stingy humourlessness which comes to rest like pitch-black coal dust and poisons the air we breathe.

There are evenings when the cold stays away. We look at each other dazed with sleep and are gripped by a strong passion. I kiss Johan's ear and he holds my head firmly between his hands. We drink too much red wine and make wild passionate love with all our longing. Later, when we are lying on the bed naked, it sometimes happens that we cry.

We find a new family therapist, a woman who does not talk about cavemen and understands why equality is important in a relationship. She pilots us carefully down winding roads of old grudges and tangled arguments.

The snow melts and it becomes spring. On our walks we see home owners cleaning their gardens. They burn leaves in small fires and hang rugs out to air. We go home and do some spring cleaning too. We mop the floors so that the whole flat smells good.

Without noticing it, life suddenly does not feel so miserable any more. The worst of the anger is gone and we do not get frostbitten as often. But deep down inside my chest there is a hard seed of bitterness which will not leave me, which makes me dwell on how bitter I am.

Yes, I am bitter. I am bitter about the fact that my first months with Sigge were so unhappy and restless. I am bitter because we could not meet each other halfway and help each other when we needed it most. That Johan failed me when I needed him the most. That I failed Johan when he needed me the most.

I am bitter because I can barely use the word betrayal when I am talking about this. I am bitter because we ended up like all couples who have children, all the ones I have read about, everyone who has told their story and witnessed how the equality disappeared when the babies came. I am bitter about realizing that we are not equals any longer – maybe we were never equals to begin with?

I am bitter about being bitter, but I do not want to be bitter.

LILL-BRITTIS IS
ENJOYING HERSELF NOW

La Quinta Park is a spa-hotel; perhaps that is why there are more retirees here than at other hotels. All the newcomers have been invited to the bar at five-thirty for a welcome drink. The German guide greets me with a long sentence in German. I nod, give her a big smile and pretend I understand what she is saying. The dining room is filled with new arrivals, contentedly sipping on their free cocktails and watching me as I try to find a glass.

I take a seat at the back so I can sneak out if need be, but I feel uncomfortable, as if everyone is staring at me. A little while later I realize that it was a mistake to come down here. I need to be alone in order to maintain the feeling of voluntary solitude, rather than partaking in group gatherings and activities. I down my free cocktail in three quick gulps and return to my own balcony. I can sit here in voluntary solitude and enjoy the quiet and the sun setting in the west, behind the mountains.

The ugly swimming pools are below me, but beyond them is a large, endless sea. An older man and an older woman in a leopard-print swimsuit are swimming around and around in the ugly pools. They are giggling. Now I can see that they are chasing each other. She catches up to him and they kiss, then they swim on.

They are so beautiful, as though they have just fallen in love. Are we going to be like that when we are older? Or will we be Dissatisfied Husband and Alcoholic Wife? I pour a glass of red wine and say cheers to myself and to the beautiful old couple in the pool.

'Lill-Brittis is enjoying herself,' I say out loud. It is an expression that comes from my mother Brittis and it has to do with wine and balconies. We were sitting on Mum's balcony one evening last summer, drinking wine, when she suddenly said, 'Now Brittis is enjoying herself,' and took a gulp of wine. She often refers to herself in the third person, as if an emotion only becomes real after she has said it out loud. My beautiful, crazy, beloved, irritating mother, who is starting to look pretty worn out. I can see that now.

Forty years of Red Prince cigarettes, full-time work at the hospital, three children and a long, unhappy marriage leaves its marks. So as a kind of tribute to Mum, my sister and I have also starting saying it when we take the first sip of wine.

'Lill-Brittis is enjoying herself now!'

The other thing which often happens when Mum is drinking wine is that she starts talking about her mother, Grandma, who was very kind, 'Far too kind', Mum says in a shaky voice. Then I know she is about to cry, because she always does when she talks about Grandma.

'She needed to take care of everyone all the time but never thought about herself. She stood up and ate at the bench while the rest of us sat around the table.'

I smile a little, because if there is one thing my mother has difficulty with, it is sitting down and relaxing at the dinner table. Sitting down and just being is impossible. Her altruism is always there, a restlessness that causes her to prepare dinner as she is clearing the table after breakfast, running in with the wash, vacuuming the hall and taking two drags on her cigarette, all while standing doubled over in front of the kitchen fan.

Sometimes when I am at home visiting I get angry and snap at her to sit down so that we can talk. It is impossible to hold a sensible conversation with someone who runs off, disappears, every other minute. Then she sighs and says yes, yes and sits down with half a cup of lukewarm coffee, takes two gulps before she is up again, at the cooker, where the potatoes have started to boil over. It is a restlessness that lives inside me too, but not in the same self-sacrificing way. Instead it is a fear that I might stop and feel something.

Isadora's mother, an eccentric red-head, says constantly that she would have been a famous artist if she had not had children, that is to say Isadora and her sisters (Gundra, Miranda, Lalah Justine and Chloe Camille!).

They grew up in a large, fourteen-room flat in Central Park West, with two studies on the north side, a library and real gold leaf on the ceiling. Isadora's mother points out that it is impossible for a woman to be both an artist and a mother. You have to choose, and since Isadora was named Isadora Zelda it is clear from early on that she is expected to choose everything her mother did not.

I guess few upbringings could have been more unlike my own. Admittedly my mother can be eccentric at times, but she is entirely devoid of artistic pretensions. Some time ago it struck me that I could not remember my mother having a hobby. Images of baking, pretzels, fish sticks, potato peeling, coffee and cigarettes being smoked next to the fan in the kitchen come to mind when I think about her.

If anything, my problem has been my parents' lack of expectation. It was not out of cruelty, but they have never been interested in what I wanted to be, whether it was a cleaner, an engineer, a postal worker, a doctor or a top lawyer. I cannot remember them ever asking me what I wanted to be when I grew up. It is this lack of interest which created an enormous need, for acknowledgement and a life unhindered by demands.

When I was twenty-one I graduated with my bachelor's degree, but I do not think they understood what it was. My God, I barely knew what it meant, just that it was an academic degree you received when you had earned enough credits at a university. A world and a language, far, far away from my own. All they understood, all *I* understood, was that I was taking a lot of strange courses in Stockholm.

It was different when I got my first long-term project placement; they understood what that meant, and Mum sent fifty kronor to Johan with a handwritten note asking him to buy a bottle of sparkling wine and celebrate that 'Sara has got her first position.' Position was a reference she understood, a job: working.

Unlike Isadora, I did not become preoccupied with an indefinable, mystical female fellowship until I had a child. That was when my mother breathed a sigh of relief, sighed a kind of sigh of normality. In her eyes a bachelor's degree was nothing compared to becoming a mother.

When Mum was twenty-six and pregnant with me, Grandma got cancer. She died when I was six months old, but it was only when I became a mother that I truly understood what it must have been like to watch your own mother dying while you were pregnant and then giving birth to your first child. How indescribably wretched it must have been to hear your chemo-poisoned mother puking in the next room while your newborn daughter is spitting up on your shoulder.

I understood this properly when I tried to talk to her about when I was born. At the time I was pregnant with Sigge and I definitely was not looking forward to the delivery. I was hoping to hear a calming story, but the only thing she could tell me was that she did not think it hurt that much, 'because the whole time I was thinking about how much pain Grandma was in and I knew that my pain would be over soon.' She did not remember any other details despite my hundred and one questions: Were you scared? Was Dad there? Were the mid-wives kind?

I have never met another woman who remembers so little of her deliveries.

One weekend when Sigge was only a few months old, Mum came to visit and we had coffee. Sigge was lying contentedly in his buggy and Mum was surprised at how calm and happy he was. She has said many times how much I cried and never slept, so much so that she finally took me to a paediatrician and asked for help. That day, when she told the story for the hundredth time, I got irritated with her.

'I was probably crying because I was anxious,' I said coldly. Mum looked at Sigge and then looked at me.

'Well, I probably couldn't bond with you because I had so much grief.'

In that moment I was prepared to forgive everything. It is so typical; she is the one I have always taken for granted. So typical that she is the one who irritates me the most, the one who was there, always. Time for a bitter bitch warning:

It is hard enough to become a mother in this damned society. The mother role and its heavy, rotten baggage is something no one should have to bear alone. Yet women are still sitting there, generation after generation, abandoned after giving birth. In the best-case scenario, a confused man is standing next to them who has been tricked into believing that he is taking his responsibility as a father by cutting the umbilical cord.

I really do not think there is much difference between becoming a mother during the 1970s or in the twenty-first century. In the beginning you are just as alone with your child as most mothers have been for centuries – despite paternity leave and daycare.

It is sad, but becoming a mother seems to be one of the most difficult undertakings when it comes to equality. It seems as though struggling against biological inequality and the even heavier weight of social and cultural inequality is just too difficult . Everything is wrapped in a longing and a love for your child which is bigger and stronger than anything else you have ever experienced. Plus, if you see the world through feminist glasses it hurts even more. It is like in the film *The Matrix*, when you have chosen the truth pill and you wake up out of your cocoon to a far uglier world than that of sleep. There is no turning back.

When we wake up and see reality as it is, a lot of people blame feminism. They twist everything around and claim that the feminist vision creates demands which are too high and contradictory, demands that break overworked women down with stress. They claim that everything was so much easier when women were housewives without the demands of work and career. Motherhood and a clean home were a woman's self-realization. Today most women work two jobs, one outside and one inside the home. Yet if we lived equally and men took just as much responsibility for the children and the home, women would not be broken down by the stress. Perhaps it is only possible to accept the difficulties if you see feminism as a resistance movement, and the only path to possible freedom. Because resistance almost always involves pain.

To say that the feelings which overwhelmed me when I became a mother were confusing is an understatement. I do not think I have ever experienced a greater joy, a greater fear, a greater thankfulness or a larger bitterness. Everything at the same time.

When it was Johan's turn to stay home everything changed, slowly but surely. Suddenly Johan was the one who knew everything, from when something was missing from the fridge or that Sigge needed a new winter coat, to which story Sigge liked the best. Suddenly I was the one who came home to a tired Johan in need of relief. I came home happy and filled with stories from the outside world.

Yet it is obvious, and has been for thousands of years, that it is the mother who should have, and often does have, the primary relationship with the children. The father's presence is more like a bonus for which we are expected to be grateful. Most fathers proudly soak up the gratitude, secure in the knowledge that they will soon return to work, confident that the average two-month paternity leave is but an interesting guest appearance.

Maybe it is the view of men's paternity leave as an *extra-ordinary feat* which makes me the most bitter bitchy, since my maternity leave is taken for granted. In the park near where we live I once saw a father wearing a dark blue t-shirt with the slogan 'On Paternity Leave'. He was walking with a baby buggy, puffed up with a self-satisfied smile just when I was the most bored with my maternity leave and hungered to go back to work. He took his baby over to the swings and swung the baby dangerously high so that his son screamed with delight. On another day, at another time, I might have found him charming.

He was one of those rare fathers who actually takes parental leave, but my generosity shone with its absence and so I stood next to him, pushing Sigge on the swing and asked where he had got the t-shirt. I do not think he noticed my bitter-ness, because he just replied cheerily that he'd got the t-shirt from the Social Insurance Office. It turned out that the Social Insurance Office had handed out the shirts to the fathers who attended its parenting classes as an encouragement to take out 'their portion of parental leave'. A nice thought and a gesture that stings my bitter bitch eyes because it shows so clearly how this society views the father's responsibility as something *extraordinary*. Despite persistent campaigns and t-shirts from different public authorities, it unfortunately seems rather impossible to get the fathers to feel or take the same responsi-bility for their children as do the mothers. Fathers in Sweden take on average twenty per cent (barely) of the parental leave. And only a small percentage of all couples share the leave equally.

The worst thing is that we go along with it, both expect-ant mothers and fathers. When I had just found out that I was pregnant with Sigge I happened to see a community programme on television. A woman in her thirties was rushing through an office area with a baby hanging on her hip. The narrator explained that IT executive Maya had been bringing her son Albert to work with her since he was born. Little Albert was crying as his mother tried to nurse him while leading a staff meeting at the same time. Then the scene changed to a demographer, a man in his sixties, who proclaimed rather seriously that there have never been fewer children born in Europe than today. This, according to the Male Demographer, was one of the worst *attacks* a society could be subjected to. He actually used the word *attack* and continued by saying that 'women's liberation' wasn't something simple, but rather something that had a string of negative effects. But unfortunately, according to the Male Demographer, you could not say this publicly without being called a reactionary.

'The core of the problem is that you can't say out loud that curbing women's education would be a good idea too,' he complained.

Then the Italian Rafaella was interviewed alongside Maya and the Male Demographer. Her ambition was to become an executive before becoming a mother. Images showed her shopping, putting on make-up, going to a job interview as well as eating at a restaurant with friends. These images were accompanied by subtitles telling us various things, like: 'The Italian woman wants to have two children, but only gets one . . .'

Nothing was said of how many children Italian men want, because it was very clear that the men had nothing to do with having children.

And the more selfish we women have become, the more society deteriorates. The Male Demographer painted horror after horror, all the grey retirees filling the streets and not enough taxpayers to take care of them.

The IT executive Maya, who sometimes worked from home, was filmed wiping Albert's snot on her sleeve while she held the telephone with the other hand, trying to hold an important conversation. Little Albert was crying the entire time, and clearly seemed upset that his mother had ambitions other than that of being a mother. The whereabouts of Little Albert's father were not interesting and never mentioned.

The fact that women in Sweden carry out seventy per cent of the unpaid housework popped up as a subtitle, as did the fact that women in Italy do ninety per cent of the same work and that there are only enough daycare places for six per cent of all Italian children. Facts that just as easily could have been presented as the explanation, or as a part of the problem.

The programme ended with a serious male voice proclaiming that, 'a large group of women born during the 1970s are not going to have time to fulfil their dreams of having two children. We have to pay the price.'

I sat there in front of the television with my mouth hanging open. I belong to that large group of egotistical women born during the 1970s, I thought to myself. Admittedly pregnant, but now I would have to pay the price because I had chosen to have children without giving up my job. Of course there would be maternity leave, a few months, but then? I do not even have a permanent job. Because I am a freelancer, what would happen when I was worn out from insomnia and could not work overtime when I needed to? And, just as men's responsibility was so strangely absent from the television programme, I realized that Johan's involvement was strangely absent from my thoughts. The message had hit its mark: children are women's responsibility. Children and career are not a good combination. Yet, if you don't choose to have children, you are selfish.

A few months later it was time to go to the parenting course under the direction of the Maternity Clinic. The breastfeeding course was lead by a woman whose last name was Tiits and the father's course was lead by a man named Dick. Tiits and Dick. Boobs and Willy. A complete coincidence.

The breastfeeding specialist's lecture was about how it was very important to breastfeed. She painted nightmarish scenarios of allergies, illness and bonding problems if you did not nurse, and made breastfeeding seem crucial for one's future relationship to one's child. That any alternative existed was not something Tiits mentioned.

In reality it was so simple – you could buy formula at the shops, you did not need to get it with a prescription from the chemist as I'd thought. This was something no one told us, nor that there are actually a lot of advantages to bottle feeding – you can take turns every other night, something which allows the mother to sleep and gives the father and child a chance to bond from the beginning, and that formula is more filling than breast milk which means the baby will sleep better at night. No one, especially not Tiits, told us this.

The Dick man began his lecture by maintaining that deep down inside, seventy per cent of all men want to have a boy, but they will only reveal this in an anonymous poll. He did not say anything about the mother's corresponding desire, or what this could result from, instead he continued by saying that paternity leave really is not all that important. What mattered was the *qualitative nearness.* Dick explained that he knew several men with their own businesses who had

77

not used a single day of their parental leave, but had still managed to be around enough during the baby's waking hours.

We took a break. I did not want to transform my suspicion that everything would work out badly into a fact. But it was already so clear that no matter what I chose it would be wrong.

Now I can laugh hysterically at Willy's lecture. What a surprise that so many couples get divorced before the child turns one. For Johan and me, it was his paternal leave which saved us. That's when he understood what it meant to take full responsibility as a father. Men should in fact take longer parental leave than women, since women have a biological head start because they have carried and given birth to their children. Men need more time to get the innate experience.

Yet I still must struggle bravely against the creeping feeling of complete egotism which rears its head whenever I choose something over Sigge. As soon as I want to work longer instead of picking Sigge up earlier from daycare. As soon as I want to go out and drink red wine one night instead of putting Sigge to bed. As soon as I want to go to Tenerife alone one week instead of being home with Sigge.

If the Male Demographer only knew how many self-absorbed feelings are housed inside me, but I can always comfort myself by reading Isadora's sensible words.

> I knew that the women who got most were the ones who demanded most out of life (and out of men) and if you acted as if you were valuable and desirable, men *found* you valuable and desirable. If you refused to be the doormat, nobody could tread on you.
>
> I knew that servile women got walked on and women who acted like queens got treated that way.

78

But no sooner had my defiant mood passed then I would be seized with desolation and despair . . .

It echoes in my head: *The one who demands the most gets the most.* In reality it is a disgusting ideology which builds on genuine egotism and a complete lack of solidarity. But sometimes I think women should be more self-serving. When it comes to women, maybe egotism can damn well work as a means of correcting the imbalance. It is just too bad that my own egotism clashes so readily with my girlish upbringing, the one which has taught me to take a step back rather than a step forward.

For example, when I'm at a party and the party's female cohorts, my fellow sisters, are running back and forth setting out the food and the wine and the dessert and the coffee and the booze while the men calmly remain sitting at the table talking and drinking more wine, to whom should I be loyal? I want to sit there too and talk and forget about the damn dishes. I want the men to get up and do their part, so that my fun, smart female friends can also gather around the table, because it's hard to carry on a conversation of any interest while you are running back and forth with the dishes, regardless of how intelligent you are. That is why men's conversations around the dinner table are often more exciting than the constantly interrupted one among the women which goes on in the kitchen. And so I sit for a bit and run around a bit and feel furious, like a traitor to my gender.

Perhaps it was this suspicion, that motherhood would devour me, make me a mother lizard without my own thoughts and time, which caused me to go to Paris when Sigge was five months old. Confused by the pain of my conversion to mother-hood, I decided to go to Paris with my best friend Sanna for a week. Before me I saw uninterrupted nights of sleep, long walks, conversations and an endless amount of much needed time for myself. Paris would be the proof that motherhood had not changed me, confirmation that I was still a free woman, with my own needs.

What I had not counted on was the enormous longing and guilt which hit me after just a few minutes on the plane. A longing that was purely physical; my heart ached and I could not focus on anything. The only thing I could think about was Sigge's scent, his warm little body next to mine, and I wondered desperately how I would survive six days in Paris.

I was deeply disappointed, because the trip was not the enjoyment for which I had hoped. By the last day I was walking on pins and needles. The public transport workers were striking so we walked around the whole day, kilometre after kilometre, from the student quarter to Montmartre and back.

Our plane was leaving at eight in the evening and we came back to the hotel around five to get our luggage and call a taxi. The man at reception just laughed. Taxi? There was a strike after all, and not a single taxi was available at such short notice. If we were really lucky we might be able to fnd one on the street, but he seriously doubted it, and there were enormous traffic jams across Paris because of the strike.

'You're going to miss your plane,' he told us. The cigarette smoke filling the lobby stung my eyes and constricted my chest. Suddenly it was difficult to breathe and I got tunnel vision. The man at the desk said that he would book a room for an additional night, just in case.

'Come on Sanna, let's go outside and try and get a taxi!'
I said, and we took our luggage and started walking.

The boulevards were packed, with cars creeping forward,
and my tunnel vision became even worse. Finally I saw a
small gap in the traffic all the way at the end of the tunnel. I
knew that I would not survive one more night without Sigge.
Missing the plane was quite simply a physical impossibility.
It just could not happen. Suddenly a taxi came creeping along
in the lane next to the footpath. I rushed over and pulled open
the door. Three men were sitting in the back seat smoking and
laughing at the surprised expression on my face. My tunnel
vision meant I could not tell which taxis were free and which
were not.

After several more minutes I managed to wave down a taxi,
and I checked first to make sure it was free. Just as the car
swung in in front of us, two young French women managed to
rush up and pull open the door before us. They could not know
that a new mother was standing there, half out of her mind,
only two metres away. With wide open eyes and clenched fists
I walked up to the women and the taxi, completely prepared
to attack.

In stumbling school-girl French I explained that we had a
flight we simply could not miss. The French women pretended
not to understand a word, and pursed their lips and rolled their
eyes. The taxi driver sat quietly and seemed to be pondering
which of us he would choose. Apparently nuance and politeness would not help here. I might as well use a sledgehammer.

'*C'est une situation du cris!*' I said as tears ran down my
cheeks.

I think I wanted to say that it was a crisis but I could not
remember the word for crisis in French. *Cris* however means

scream. This is a screaming situation, which in a way it was. And apparently it made an impression on the taxi driver who started dismissing the women in hot-tempered French. They swore and made foul gestures at our wonderful taxi driver whom I felt as though I would love for ever. He had saved my life!

Another tremulous thirty minutes in the back seat remained while we snaked our way through the traffic jam. I gripped Sanna's hand the whole time. She tried to calm me down and repeatedly said that we would not miss our flight, but it was not until we got out on the motorway and the traffic disappeared that I really started to believe we would make it.

When I got home that night I lay down next to Sigge in our bed and looked at him. His little mouth, which was smiling in his sleep, his small breaths through his nose. After a while he woke up and saw my eyes and smiled. I stroked his hair and cheek and kissed him on the ear. Beloved, beloved little child! He soon fell back asleep between me and Johan, yet I lay awake for a long time and cried about being so confused, that I was doing everything wrong, that nothing turned out the way I wanted it to, that everything hurt so damn much all the time.

In hindsight I can understand why I was forced to go to Paris, even if it is pitiful that I was compelled to carry on proving things like that to myself; that I did not have the peace simply to be. But I became bitter bitchy and conspiratorial when I thought about Johan being gone five days a week for two months when Sigge was only three months old. And of course he longed to be home, but not in that desperate, tunnel vision way I had in Paris.

There are obviously differences between me and Johan, and I think about why that is. I know that Johan loves Sigge more than anything else, but it seems as though, unlike me, he can love without guilt. As if motherhood is so horribly weighed down with duty and the sublimation of all personal needs that it will always clash with the tiniest exertion of freedom.

It makes me jealous; I want to love without guilt in the way that men do. Yes, I want to have my cake and eat it too. I want to be able to work, party, travel, be alone once in a while *and* be a mother to a beloved child. Admittedly, the self-sacrificing mother lives on inside many of us as a contradictory and hated ideal image, but she lives in stiff competition with a lot of other ideals. Thank goodness! She even has to struggle in order to survive there inside of us, because the women's movement has slowly but surely made it possible for my generation of women to choose something more than just being a mother. Some of us do not even want to be mothers.

PRAYING TO GOD
(1983)

There is a ping-pong table behind the hotel where we run around and around, only stopping to drink Fanta or eat some dill crisps that Mum has set out for us. The grown-ups are sitting at a table a little way off, sipping on drinks. I hear Dad getting noisy and Mum is quiet. Their friends Lars and Ann-Marie are laughing about something and then I hear Mum laugh as well, a short little laugh. I continue running, hitting the ping-pong ball every time it comes my way. I am good at knockout ping-pong. We played it during every break in the school gym all spring long.

We have been swimming all day, far out into the sea, which is shallow a long way out. We swim over deep chasms and up on sandbanks that are suddenly there, making us touch the bottom. Dad told us that underwater currents can form and pull you down into the deep. On the way back to land I am scared as we swim over the deep parts, but nothing happens and afterwards it is nice to lie in the sun and warm up.

We are staying in a house next to the hotel with blue-striped wallpaper and wicker chairs; pictures of the sea and seagulls hang on the walls. A tall, skinny man is staying in the room next to ours. We were sitting in the common area outside our room when he came out of his and went down the stairs. Then he switched the light in the hall on and off at least ten times before he finally went out the door.

'It's called an obsession,' says Dad, and explains that some people who are mentally ill get the idea that they are going to die if they do not turn the light on and off a certain number of times before they go out. I think about the fact that I force myself to take four steps on the stairs before the door at school closes. If I can manage that, then I know that my heart will not stop beating that night. But now I think I am going to stop. I do not want to be sick like that man, tall and skinny and alone.

Suddenly Mum is standing at the ping-pong table with the baby buggy in which my little brother is sleeping.

'Come on, it's time to go to our room!' she says in a harsh voice. I can see Dad still sitting at the table with their friends.

'Isn't Dad coming?' I ask.

'No, he's coming later,' she says, and hurries us up.

Dad does not look at us when we leave and I know that they have had a fight. When we get to our house it is plunged in darkness and I hope the crazy man is not standing somewhere in the dark outside our room. It is just us and him in the whole house. I am scared but I finally fall asleep after Mum shows me that she has locked the door.

I wake to the sound of Mum and Dad's bed creaking, a rhythmic thumping. After a few seconds I hear Mum say, 'If you don't stop I'm going to scream for help!' I lie on my camp bed thinking that the only other person in the whole house is the crazy man. I lie perfectly still and do not know what I am supposed to do. Now my heart really is going to stop beating. I feel it in my whole body, but just as I am placing my hand over my chest to check, my sister throws herself out of bed. She turns on the light and says, 'What are you doing?' with a loud, angry voice.

I see Dad roll off Mum and get up and put on his underpants. He has a hard time balancing but manages to get dressed. He does not make a sound and neither does Mum. He takes the car keys and his wallet and puts them in his pocket too. Just as he is about to walk out the door he catches sight of my sister's pink wallet, pours out her money and puts it in his pocket.

'That's my money!' Kajsa screams and starts crying. 'Mum, he's taking my money!' When Dad has left, Mum says that she will get more money tomorrow.

'You have to try and sleep now!' says Mum.

The next morning I hear Mum trying to explain to Ann-Marie that Dad disappeared during the night.

'He was so nasty,' Mum says. 'He just took the car and left.'

Ann-Marie asks her something and Mum replies, 'I don't know. But he was so nasty to me!'

She does not say anything else and Ann-Marie does not ask. We eat breakfast and I see the tall, skinny man sitting alone at a table further away. Maybe he heard? We pack our things and go to the train station. Lars and Ann-Marie and their kids are already at the beach so they cannot come with us and say goodbye. All of us are embarrassed, I think, but maybe Ann-Marie did not understand what it meant, the part about Dad being so nasty to Mum.

Dad always pays for everything and Mum always has to ask him for money, then he gets out his wad of bills and gives her some. But last night I saw him take his thick, black wallet with him. I saw him take Kajsa's money too.

'Do we have enough money for the train tickets?' I ask Mum at the station.

'Yes, you don't have to worry!' she says and buys sweets for me and Kajsa.

We travel for several quiet hours through summery Sweden, filled with yellow fields and thick forests. I am sweating but I do not get sick like I always do in the car.

'Are you going to get a divorce now?' I ask Mum.

'No, we aren't,' Mum says, but I do not believe her.

When we get home Dad is sitting in the back yard, smoking. I am relieved that he has not wrecked the car during the night and died, but I do not say hello and I refuse to look him in the eye.

I walk to the park to see if any of my friends are there. On summer evenings everyone who is at home plays cops and robbers. It is the best game I know, but there are not any friends playing outside tonight. Everyone is away on holiday, just like we were.

After a while I go home. I can tell that Mum and Dad are happy again. Mum is making rhubarb fool and setting out sandwiches for dinner as though nothing happened. I see her in the kitchen, back to me, and I do not understand her. I do not know her.

I still have not said one word to Dad and I do not say anything now either. He tries to make eye contact but I turn away from him and go to bed. For the first time in my life I wish they would get a divorce. But they do not.

At night I pray to God, asking for all kinds of things, things I want to have, things I want to have happen. It feels good knowing that he is up there watching and listening to me.

'The best way to honour God is to sing for him,' says our Christian primary school teacher. I immediately join the Christian choir at the free church close to where we live. Several of my classmates are also members and every Wednesday evening we sing in God's honour.

'It's pronounced AAAAAva, not EEEEva. You can call me Äva,' explains the choir director. She is big and fat and speaks with a Värmland accent. I love singing all the hymns and I sing in a high-pitched voice. I like my voice, but sometimes Äva tells me not to sing so loud.

'You're drowning everyone else out, Sara!' Then I sing a bit more softly.

> This is the day
> This is the day
> The Lord has made
> The Lord has made
> Let us rejoice and be glad in it
> Let us rejoice and be glad in it
> We thank the Lord, yes we thank the Lord

I do so want to become Christian. At church there is a fellowship I watch with a hunger inside, I can almost feel it. Everyone in the choir except me has parents who are members of the congregation. But each night I hope and pray to God that Mum and Dad will become Christians and join the church, that they will stop fighting and be nice.

Dear God, I pray, make Mum and Dad come and see me sing in the choir. But they do not come, and every Sunday during the service Äva lets everyone else sing a solo except for me. Finally I ask if I will get to sing a solo one day.

'Yes, maybe one day. There's nothing wrong with your voice Sara, but the others have parents in the church who want to see their children sing. Do you understand that it's important for them to get to sing, when their parents are here to listen?'

I understand, but everything has started to hurt. There is a burning sensation in my eyes and my tights are making me itch. I stop singing in the choir and I start drawing instead. Big, fat Ävas who change into angels and fly up to God. Sometimes they lose their wings and fall down and die.

I draw a picture of me as a princess with a Daddy king who is kind, and a beautiful Mummy queen. They love me more than anything else and every day we stroll through our large garden and talk to each other. The king is interested. He asks me what I like best, drawing or singing? Drawing, I say.

Mummy queen is heartbroken. 'My sweet child, you sing so fantastically! You must never stop singing!'

But Daddy king says that I can both draw and sing.

I sit at my desk for hours and draw and draw, pictures depicting stories that make me happy. I take an especially good drawing of the three of us in our castle garden down to Mum and Dad. To Mum and Dad, I have written at the top.

'Here. I drew it.'

'Oh, well isn't that nice!' Mum says as she is doing the dishes.

'But you didn't look.'

'Oh, but of course I did,' Mum says, and turns a little more. She cannot take it because her hands are wet with dishwater.

I put the drawing next to the telephone and hope they will hang it on the refrigerator. But it remains lying there and one day I crumple it into a tiny ball, and throw it pointedly into the rubbish.

'Why don't you ever see anything?' I scream and run up to my room, tears streaming.

'My goodness what was that?' I hear Dad ask Mum.

I think about all the Christians I know. My best friend Mariella and her family, they seem happy. I have never seen her parents argue or say horrible things to each other. Mariella's mother is my day mother, so every day after school Mariella and I go to her house. Sometimes we get rosehip soup with ice cream as a snack and Mariella's mother never seems stressed. She sits down at the table with us and asks how our day has been.

One day she grabs hold of me, pulls me towards her and gives me a long, hard hug.

'Mmm . . .' she says and smells my hair, just as if she is enjoying it.

'Why are you doing that?' I ask, perplexed.

'You look as though you need a hug,' she says, and smiles at me.

I do not smile back, I do not want to show the tears which are going to come at any moment. Instead I say, 'OK,' and go upstairs to Mariella's room.

Sometimes I fantasize that Mum and Dad die in a car accident and I am adopted by Mariella's parents, or by my teacher. She is also a Christian, and she is one of the best people I know. She knows so much and tells us long stories from the Bible. I know some of them because of *The Children's Bible* Grandma gave me for Christmas. I have read about Jesus's goodness and about a lot of crazy, evil people who did not know anything. My teacher leads the juniors at the free church and almost the whole class is there every Wednesday night. The ones whose parents are members of the church have the highest standing with her and I dream about Mum and Dad joining too. I wonder what it feels like to meet the teacher every Sunday after the service?

All Christians seem to be happy all the time and I am sure Mum and Dad would be happy too if they became Christians. I write in my light-blue diary in my best handwriting: *Dear God. Make Mum and Dad Christian. Also thanks for being such a good God, because you let it snow. It's pretty.*

But God probably does not read small, light-blue diaries because Mum and Dad never become Christians. They argue and I know they are unhappy. Dad is gone for several weeks at a time and Mum is so busy preparing meals, doing the dishes and vacuuming that she does not have the time or energy for anything else.

One day Mum wants all of us to go to a real photographer and have a studio portrait taken. I want to go because I am thinking about *The Cosby Show* on TV. The Cosby family are always happy; Christian and happy. I so badly want our family to look happy in a photograph. Mum is beaming and she is trying to make me and my sister look nice. She makes a frilly blouse for each of us out of an old sheet. The frill is stiff and I can see that the seams are uneven, because Mum was in a hurry when she made the blouses, but I do not want to argue with her when she is so happy. The night before the appointment she decides to trim our fringes; the hair has been hanging in our eyes and should have been trimmed a long time ago. She takes a pair of scissors and zigzags her way through our hair. It is uneven because Mum cannot cut hair, especially fringes. We still do not say anything, we do not even fight with each other, but continue to be nice. It is unusual to see Mum so happy and carefree. She stands in front of the mirror and puts on her new pink lipstick.

In the morning Dad does not want to come with us. We are sitting around the table eating toast with orange marmalade and Mum is pouring Dad's coffee.

'Please,' Mum pleads dejectedly. 'We've booked a time and everything.'

But Dad does not budge and says he is too tired. Mum stands at the kitchen bench with her back to us and Dad lights a cigarette and leans back in his chair, and I cannot sit there any longer. I go out into the hall where I catch sight of myself in the mirror and I start crying because I see how uneven my bangs are, how ugly I am. My sister comes out and asks why I am crying and I yell that I am crying because we are all so damned ugly, every one of us.

'Mum!' Kajsa yells. 'Mum! Sara said that I'm ugly!'

She stands in front of the mirror next to me and starts crying when she sees herself.

'Now you'd better calm down!' Mum yells from the kitchen as she picks my little brother up from his high chair.

'You can sit there and sulk,' I hear her say to Dad, 'but the rest of us are going to the photographer's. And I'm taking the car!'

Silence falls and Kajsa and I stop crying. The car is his, and Mum almost never gets to borrow it. He has said so many times, because women are terrible drivers and besides, he is the one who is paying for it. Mum could never afford a car with her puny wages. I know because Dad often says that Mum's salary does not make a difference.

We listen tensely after the outburst, but it is still quiet in the kitchen and Mum comes out and tells us to put on our shoes because we are leaving now. So we get in the car without Dad, and suddenly everything feels festive again. Mum puts on the radio which is playing Carola and we sing along to her 'Foreigner' all the way to the photographer's.

We have to stand against a dark blue background with our little brother between us. Mum does not want to be in the picture because Dad is not there so it becomes a photo of us siblings. Afterwards we each get a hotdog from the stand at the square. It is a warm summer day and we continue being happy and getting along the rest of the afternoon and evening, even though Dad is gone when we get home.

The photos arrive a few days later and we really look horrible, all three of us. Dishevelled, with crooked hair and sad eyes. We are smiling stiffly, even our two-year-old brother's smile looks fake. But Mum is really happy and frames the photos and hangs them on the wall. She wraps a few of them for Christmas, presents for Grandma and other relatives.

It is August and there are a few weeks left of the summer holiday. The evenings are warm and Mum and our neighbour Gunilla sit outside on the tiny patio at the front of our terrace house a lot, smoking and drinking Rosita while we run past and grab a fistful of dill crisps from the bowl on the table. We are playing cops and robbers and I cannot run very fast, but I am good at throwing myself in the bushes and hiding while the others chasing me just run by without noticing me.

This is the summer in which I discover that I cannot run around naked any more. We are at a swimming place and I am wearing the bottom part of my suit but not the top which covers my budding breasts. I am nine years old and no one says anything, but suddenly I know it. Maybe I can feel the stares?

I stand in front of the mirror in the hall a lot and look at myself. I try and understand how someone can be as terribly ugly as I am. My hair is rat coloured and hangs in worn wisps that barely reach my shoulders. I pout my lips and open my eyes wide so that they will look bigger, try different expressions, but nothing helps. I know this already but I cannot keep from trying, in the hopes that something will have changed.

One morning, as I am standing in front of the mirror, trying out my hair in a pony tail, Dad comes and stands next to me. I am embarrassed but I can see that he sees me. His eyes are a warm brownish-yellow just like mine. I have inherited his eye colour.

'You look pretty with your hair up,' he says, and continues to look at me.

'Nah . . .' I say hesitantly. It feels strange and unfamiliar.

'You do. Now I can see your pretty face!' he says, and walks into the kitchen to light his first cigarette of the morning.

I remain standing there with my mouth gaping, amazed at what has just happened.

My dad said I was pretty! I look at myself in the mirror and put my hair in a pony tail. I try to see if what he said is true, if I have a pretty face. Maybe it is just a little bit true? Maybe I am just a little bit less ugly with my hair up?

Sometimes small miracles occur, like Dad coming with us to the pool one Sunday. Usually it is Mum who comes with us. She swims laps while we play in the children's pool nearby. I love the pool and sitting in the hot sauna afterwards with all of the naked women who are chatting and sweating.

This Sunday when Dad comes with us he plays with us in the children's pool. He is a crocodile swimming under the water and chasing us. We scream with delight and exultation. It is so amazing that he is playing with us and that it is finally happening, now, just once.

A constant longing, a constant frustration spreads and infects, making me and my sister fight a lot. I have scratch marks high up on my arms and a teacher points at my scratches and asks if we have a cat. Another time when we are fighting I grab Kajsa's fingers so hard they break and she has to go to the hospital and they are set in a plaster cast. Then I am genuinely ashamed but I cannot make myself apologize.

It is a constant disdain in a downward spiral, which begins with Dad making fun of Mum.

'It's "accept" not "assept"! Learn to speak properly for once!' he says with an evil grin on his face, and Mum, who never sticks up for herself, falls silent as she always does.

His disdain is infectious and for a long, long time I believe Dad when he says that Mum is stupid. Even Mum seems to think so. Every now and then he pops out of the cloud of smoke that constantly encircles him.

'Dad, please don't smoke when we're watching TV!' Kajsa and I ask with our noses buried in our shirts in order to escape the rank, sticky smell.

'Listen up! I'm the one who pays for everything. This is my house and I'll smoke as much as I damn well please!' he replies angrily, and continues taking long drags on his White Prince.

He is our almighty father, feared and admired. Someone to long for your entire life.

Always poor posture, always something that is itching, and I do not change until I have turned eleven and that is when Cecilia joins our class. Cissi has long, red hair and nostrils that flare when she laughs. For some reason, which I never understand, Cissi wants to be my friend. She laughs at all of my jokes and thinks I am the funniest person in the class. She waits for me after school so we can walk home together. From that point on she is my best friend for life.

With Cissi at my side I finally build up the courage to be

myself. We sit in my room and fantasize about Don Johnson and Sylvester Stallone, about a life in Hollywood where we are loved and admired. Sometimes we switch and fantasize about Jesper and Adam in our class, on whom all of the girls have crushes. With Cissi anything can happen and it does, too. One day, when we are fantasizing about Jesper and Adam ringing the doorbell, we suddenly hear the doorbell ring, then the sound of quick steps and my door is opened by Jesper and Adam. Happily we go out into the magic summer evening and on to the jungle gym in the playground, where we kiss our princes.

That summer we discover the paper mill which is close to our neighbourhood. It is surrounded by a high fence with barbed wire on top, but some of the boys show us a hole we can sneak through. There are huge piles of newspaper in there which we climb on and the mill is filled with older boys who watch us, wide-eyed. We find magazines in the paper piles. It is just a matter of taking what we want. There are tons of porn magazines, too, which the boys collect and put in their plastic bags.

It is against the law to be in there and sometimes someone yells that the security guards are coming. Everyone runs and the boys show us secret holes among the paper bales where you can hide until the guards have disappeared. We sit there close to each other, close to the boys, and we hear the dogs barking below us. We are almost grown up and everything is dangerous and exciting, just like Hollywood.

Late in the evening, when it is almost dark, some of the boys want us to look at their porn magazines. It is the first time I see what female genitalia looks like from below. In one of the pictures there is a woman with her legs spread apart and there, inside her body, a vacuum cleaner hose has been stuck. I look at her eyes to see if it is painful, but her eyelids are half closed, as if she is falling asleep.

In another picture there is a woman using her fingernails to pull open her labia, revealing small gold rings, three on each one. Cissi and I sit quietly and look. The boys have also become quiet and it is dark and I want to go home. Why does everything have to be so disgusting? We walk silently past the terrace houses where we live. Thick mucus in my throat makes it hard to breathe and I have to stop and spit every few feet. Cissi clears her throat and spits too, out of sympathy, but we still cannot talk to each other. At home Dad is sitting watching *The Macahans* on TV. As usual Mum is busy in the kitchen with her restless movements.

I sit down on the sofa next to Dad and see Zeb Macahan shoot an injured horse with his revolver. The horse looks frightened and does not understand why Zeb has hurt him. The eyelids are half closed and Zeb is stroking the horse on its head and talking soothingly. Finally the horse stops fighting and his body becomes completely still. I look at the dead horse and suddenly I am sobbing loudly. My body is shaking and I cannot stop the tears which are pouring down my cheeks and throat.

Dad looks at me in surprise and puts his arm around my shoulders. It feels unfamiliar, he has not touched me in so long. I cannot remember the last time he hugged me.

'There there, sweetheart. The horse was injured, it would have died eventually anyway,' he says, and I hear how his voice sounds thick and tearful too, and then I cry even more.

And I never want to stop crying. I just want to sit there in his arms and be comforted for ever.

FAMILY JOY

The woman with the cock-coloured outfit ate breakfast alone again today. She looked sad – until now she has looked a bit more drunk and detached. After a while her German husband came and sat down. Then she brightened and quickly got up to get a cup of German herbal tea for him. I saw how she carefully picked through the tea blends. I heard a short *Danke*, and then they continued eating in silence.

I cannot stop. My observations just become darker and darker. I try and look away, read my book, take off my sunglasses and think about something else but it does not help. Besides, after a few days I have started feeling like I know some of the couples here. It is a feeling that makes me stare even more openly.

Another group of Germans has sat down at the table next to mine. One of the women came before her husband and set a cup of coffee at one seat, and said hello to two friends who had already started eating. Then she went to get the rest of her breakfast. While she was gone her husband came, with his plate piled high with bread and toppings. Without hesitating he sat down at the place where she had put her coffee, let out a small *mm* . . . and took a gulp, as if the coffee had been put there for him. Why not? Of course the coffee was for him.

When the wife came back with her food she did not let on that he had made a mistake. She did not smile indulgently or point it out. She turned around quietly and got a new cup for herself.

Some of the couples look reasonably happy. Some of them are actually enjoying their parallel loneliness, while others have merely accepted the lack of contact and their parallel lives. When I interviewed one of my great idols, Suzanne Brøgger, I remember how infinitely disappointed I was by her speech about 'gratitude', which she claimed she had experienced in her later years.

'Should we just settle then?' I asked, frustrated.

'Yes, why not?' she said. She was the one who had written several wonderfully brave, self-revelatory books about not settling, the one who has always studied how to live one's life in the most interesting and least unhappy way. It was she who had written the most beautiful and sad thing I had ever read about the difficulties of coupling: that coupling is an organized form of an unlived life. A string of non-meetings. But here at the hotel in Tenerife, I am prepared to believe that maybe that is how it is with contentedness, or gratitude; that it comes with age. You are quite simply content with less.

I can go along with 'gratitude', in the sense of having the peace to stop and rest and look at what you have, to see that wealth is within your reach. When you have imagined that the grass is greener on the other side, you have usually discovered that this is not the case. A certain talent is required in order to realize what you have.

Though I am not really sure that is what Suzanne Brøgger meant.

It can be risky to meet your idol in the flesh, especially if her name is Suzanne Brøgger and she has written books depicting the nuclear family's hell with such feeling that she may have inspired hundreds of women to take action and actually get divorced. And if I am going to be honest, I also wanted a lot of personal answers from this wise woman. Answers to questions about my own little marital hell in which I was then living.

When I read her book *Deliver Us from Love* for the first time, I immediately adopted her as my universal dream mother. The one who, in contrast to my biological mother, would never bake a single cursed bread roll, but to whom you could talk. My copy of her book is filled with underlining and exclamation marks, and I know some sections by heart. So when the opportunity to interview Suzanne Brøgger presented itself I grabbed it. I wanted to know what she was thinking some thirty years after writing *Deliver Us from Love*, what she thought about the children of the 1970s who had got married while she and several other women from her generation had paved the way for an entirely different way of life. Why the traditional church wedding was more popular now than ever among my generation.

I knew that even Brøgger had gotten married and had children. So as I rang the doorbell of her flat I expected to encounter a duality similar to my own; that the ideas she had then would not really be the same today, even if I might hope that they were.

She opened the door and I registered that what I had heard about her beauty was true, as well as her predilection for leopard-print clothing and red lipstick. And I thought that the best thing might be to have several different kinds of mothers, the bread baking, fish-stick smelling, and the eccentric, intellectual, sexual, because a combination of the two is not imaginable.

She smiled and gave me a pair of golden ballet slippers, no joke. I smiled back stupidly and wished I was just as magnificent as she was. She served tea in beautiful cups with gold edges and I turned on the tape recorder and began.

'Why do you think so little has happened in the thirty years since you wrote *Deliver Us from Love*? Why do you think my generation has run off and got married?'

Suzanne took a sip of tea and thought for a few seconds. 'Well, maybe because these waves go up and down and forwards and backwards and every generation rebels against the previous one,' she replied.

'So us having gone and got married should be seen only as a reaction against you?' I asked, and stared hard at her mouth as if the answer that would soon appear was of decisive importance, which it was in a way.

'I mean that if you have children, you will always have the problem of the triangle father-mother-child, and so I think that each individual must adapt, and external factors do not mean that much. But when you're young you think that maybe a certain lifestyle is vital to the success of your life. On the other hand, things are not as secure as they once were, both in the cities and in the country. This can be viewed as an expression of fear: in an insecure world with terrorism and lack of control, you focus on the nuclear family.'

I tested my theories, that love has been exploited so that women give and men take, that married women have more mental health issues than their unmarried counterparts, and so on. Suzanne nodded a little but did not say anything. I asked why there are so few stories, almost none, about happy women who have chosen solitude over marriage. Suzanne sighed but looked at me kindly and said that free love is just as big a problem as love in a steady relationship. That was not the answer I wanted and I tapped my golden-slippered feet, looked at the gold on the teacup and thought that somehow gold was standing in the way.

Suzanne Brøgger, on the other hand, was probably used to people feeling disappointed in her, and I feel embarrassed when I think back to how she must have been smiling inside at the sight of poor desperate me.

'How do you want to live, then?' Suzanne countered, and I realized that she was growing tired of this interview and the interviewer in particular.

'How?' I asked, in order to win some time.

'Yes . . . ?' said Suzanne.

'I don't know, I'm thinking about it,' I replied, pitifully.

'Well, you have all the freedom to do that,' Suzanne replied, and smiled. And in that moment she became a bit like the wise mum I hoped she would be, but now I felt awkward and exposed and tears started to form in my eyes.

I did not want to sit there and cry at her kitchen table, so instead I quickly returned to the safe role of interviewer.

'Do you think patriarchy has a need for marriage?' I asked.

This was one of my biggest theories and pet projects, that patriarchy could be likened to a super ideology, a kind of religion which has affected us down to the tiniest element, and as part of this ideology, we were persuaded to marry as a means of smothering all struggle and rebellion. As a result, most stories – movies, television, books – are about longing for romantic love, which is made whole through marriage. A false image, which never includes the dark side, abuse, rape and unpaid, disgusting, boring household chores.

But Suzanne did not agree. 'I actually don't think the inherent patriarchy in our culture is that strong today. We certainly carry some traces within ourselves, but not compared to the power men in Muslim families have over their women. Then you can talk about patriarchy!'

I always become suspicious when people start talking about how much worse it is in other cultures. All too often I hear people say it in order to smooth over the injustices in Sweden, an argument that we should satisfy ourselves with the success we have had. Now I started wondering if Danish MP Pia Kjærsgaard's racist anti-immigration stance had affected Dane Suzanne Brøgger, of all people.

'But I still think we live in a patriarchal society,' I said.

'Well, everything is relative, but you can live the way you want without being killed. They can't. I just mean that if the patriarchy still exists then it exists inside us in the form of self-oppressing mechanisms,' Suzanne replied.

'Though I think it quite clearly exists in both Sweden and Denmark too, in the form of all of the women being beaten to death by their husbands and all of the rapes. Patriarchal oppression is real and is felt by most women,' I persisted, because as I've said, this is one of my passions. Oppression might take different forms in different countries, but the origin is the same: patriarchy. Or the gender power balance – men's power over women, or whatever you want to call it.

'Yes, that's true, and men take revenge on feminism's success. Violence against women is more common now than ever before,' she said, and I was filled with a childish delight because we finally agreed on something.

But then I ruined everything by asking if she knew any happy couples. Because in *Deliver Us from Love*, she states that one of the reasons she did not believe in coupling was that she had simply never known any happy couples. Suzanne replied that she was herself an example of a happy twosome, working sufficiently well that she would want to continue with it for the time being.

'But,' she said, 'you probably get better at living together when you're older. A concept like gratitude comes later, as you get older.'

'Do you feel grateful?' I asked.

'Yes,' Suzanne replied, simply.

'What are you grateful for?' I asked.

'I'm grateful that I'm alive and that there is tenderness and that no one I love is sick or dying. That's what I'm grateful for,' Suzanne replied, and looked happy.

I looked down into my teacup because I was ashamed that I could not hide my disappointment any longer. I had expected so much from our meeting, and not that she would sit there and be grateful.

Maybe she did not see my disappointment, or she misinterpreted it, or maybe she just did not give a damn (respectfully) about my expectations, because she started to tell me happily about a song she was working on, about a man who could do forty-eight things.

'What kind of forty-eight things?' I asked. 'Well, fix my fax, cut my trees, fix my computer, fill up the car and help me find my way . . . I've forgotten but there were forty-eight things, and I think that's enough. Forty-eight things. That's good,' said Suzanne.

Our tea had grown cold now and I felt as though I no longer knew what we were babbling on about. I began to wonder if I had understood her Danish. Maybe we really agreed on everything but had misunderstood each other. A simple confusion of languages? Regardless of the reason, my head was spinning and it was time to wrap things up.

'Yeah, maybe forty-eight things are enough,' I said, interested, even though I could not have agreed less, instead I thought it sounded like total rubbish. Maybe there was a symbolic inter-pretation of the forty-eight things which I did not get?

'It's just that I feel an impatience; that we should have come further in the thirty years since *Deliver Us from Love* came out,' I tried one last time.

'But maybe it's a matter of not enough having happened with men,' Suzanne said.

'Yes, we should have a look at them!'

'Or they should have a look at themselves, because quite a lot has happened with women but not that much has happened with men. It seems as though they think they don't need to do anything. But taking up that struggle in marriage is too hard. It's one thing raising children, it's another if you need to raise the men too. No, that's just too much!'

I suddenly thought I understood her vision: it had to do with the old honourable play between private practice and universal theory. The play between society and individual, with a little bit of resignation to top it off.

When I got back to my hotel room at Nyhavn I was cheerful again. Although I could not get over my embarrassment and dis-appointment, I felt charitable. Who was I to think (demand!) that she should serve all of the answers on a plate? Suzanne Brøgger has every right to step back and live her life with all of the contradictory feelings coupling involves. How embarrass-ing that I had the guts to sit there and almost feel wronged just because she feels grateful!

I go back to my hotel room and sit on the balcony for a while and breathe in the clear morning air. It is cloudy today so I decide to take the bus to the city where the travel agency is organizing a guided city tour.

One of the couples sits next to me on the bus. They are not talking to each other. She is looking in a brochure and he is staring straight ahead. He suddenly turns his head and catches a glimpse of his reflection in the bus window.

'*Ah meine frisur ist kaput!*' he says, and laughs while running his fingers through his thin, old man's hair.

The wife is ecstatic at this possible opening and she starts laughing hysterically, an appreciative but hollow sounding laugh. She looks around at the rest of us on the bus to see if anyone else has understood this great comedic achievement, but no one seems to have got the joke.

Then she laughs even louder and you understand how unusual it must be in her world to have her husband crawl out of his surliness and open up a bit. And you know that when he does do it, it is important to be there with an appreciative laugh in order to get him to stick around as long as possible. Quite right, it looks as though he is satisfied with this confirmation. They start talking about the harbour, which we can see from the bus now.

My heart aches a bit. I recognize the pattern from several relationships around me, including my own. How the women are tiptoeing around, constantly inquisitive, prepared to either parry or laugh loud and appreciatively. How much energy does this take?

The psychoanalyst Joan Riviere, in her essay, 'Womanliness as a Masquerade', published in 1929, talks about how skilled, professional women would make themselves appear more stupid when men were around. They did everything so that the men would not feel vulnerable to competition and so that their own femininity would not be questioned. To a certain degree this probably holds true even today, but here on the bus down to Puerto de la Cruz, I think today's masquerade of womanliness is more about putting up with closed-off men and pretending that everything is fine by laughing loudly at their jokes.

The bus stops next to a busy shopping centre in the city and everyone gathers and waits for the guide. We set off and I think how good this is, because it will keep my Stockholm snobbery at bay. I am walking with sixteen recent retirees, all of whom look like they have just returned from a campervan holiday. They are from Germany, Landvetter and Karlskrona and they are rather wonderful. They look excited at the thought of taking part in an adventurous outing: a guided city tour in Puerto de la Cruz. I can feel my heart swell and the sun makes me happy, as does the fact that people are allowed to be this nerdy. It feels liberating and relaxed.

Two Danish families with children are also part of the group. The children are toddlers and the parents look my age. The mothers are pushing the buggies and the fathers walk slowly, falling further and further behind. Finally they end up at the back of the group, with me. They joke with each other, watching me the whole time to see if I have noticed what fun lads they are. But since I do not understand Danish, I do not understand how funny they are; instead I become irritated by their typical, public escape from their family. I consider the opposite scenario: two mothers slowing down and ending up next to the single, thirty-year-old man at the back of the group, with whom they then start flirting and trying to make contact while their husbands are walking twenty feet ahead with the buggies.

'What's your name?' one of them says in guttural Danish.

'Sorry, I don't speak Danish,' I reply.

'Oh, what's your name?' he continues in English.

'Sue Ellen,' I answer.

'Oh nice,' he says. 'My name is Mads.'

'Oh, nice,' I say.

'And my name is Henrik,' says the other. 'Are you here alone on holiday?'

'No I'm here for work. I'm an actor and we're here performing a play called *Dallas* tomorrow at the casino.'

'Oh, nice,' Mads replies, and I get the feeling that their English is not very good.

'Can we come and watch you?' Henrik asks, and looks pleased at his boldness.

'Yes of course. It's open to everyone. Tomorrow at nine o'clock in the casino.'

Henrik and Mads start speaking excitedly to each other in Danish and I can make out two women's names, 'Anne' and something that sounds like 'Rue'. I suspect they are the wives' names, and I wonder if it is really possible that *Dallas* was not shown on TV in Denmark in the 1980s?

'OK, we'll come tomorrow and maybe we can have a drink with you?' says Henrik.

'Or two drinks . . . or three . . . ?' Mads fills in and laughs at his hilarious joke.

'OK,' I say. 'See you tomorrow!'

Henrik and Mads grin confidently and speed up so that they have soon caught up with their wives, Anne and Rue. For a split second I feel guilty; there is no way Henrik and Mads could know that one of my favourite pastimes is to lie to men who are screwing around. But the feeling disappears when I see

Henrik put his arm possessively around Anne and Mads kiss Rue tenderly on the cheek. They can stand outside the casino for a while and wonder what happened to *Dallas*.

I skip the group lunch which has been organized for the guided tour and sneak off and find my own café. I order grilled sword-fish, beer and an espresso. I let the sun warm my face as I continue to read about Isadora.

She and Bennett have just arrived at the university in Vienna where the conference will be held. Isadora is angry with Bennett because he is not a stranger on a train – the zipless fuck – because he does not smile, does not talk to her. She is angry because he makes her appointments with gynaecologists and analysts but never buys her flowers, angry because he does not kiss her, or grab her bum.

And this is when she meets Adrian. Her longed-for zipless fuck, a fantasy she has created about a guilt-free fuck which has nothing to do with buttons needing to be undone.

> The zipless fuck is absolutely pure. It is free of ul-terior motives. There is no power game. The man is not 'taking' and the woman is not 'giving'. No one is attempting to cuckold a husband or humiliate a wife. No one is trying to prove anything or get any-thing out of anyone. The zipless fuck is the purest thing there is. And it is rarer than the unicorn.

To my great sadness, neither Isadora nor I have experienced a zipless fuck.

A few unsuccessful opportunities presented themselves when I was single, but the guilt was always there in the form of an unspoken question about whether it would become something more. I felt guilty about not wanting anything more, guilty about having taken the initiative for a zipless fuck. I felt guilty because that damned age old rule still counts if you are a woman: be hunted, do not do the hunting.

How many times have I made a mistake there? Ever since I was twelve and excitedly rubbed myself against Fredrik L, all the way up to the men of the art academy when I was twenty-one. Sanna and I, in true kamikaze fashion, used to go up to men at the bar and ask straight out if they had a hot one. Almost none of them ever did. In any case not one they wanted to stick inside us. Or if someone came up and asked if we had a light, we said no, but we did have a burning clit. I suspect we wanted to see what it felt like to be just as fearless and cocky as the men. We had a blast, laughed coarsely, loved ourselves and hated all of the quiet, mysterious girls the boys seemed to flock around.

It hardly ever worked.

It only worked once and I married him. Johan was the first one to laugh when I asked if he had a hot one. In my intoxicated arrogance I interpreted his laugh as an invitation.

'Let's go and snog!' I said, and pushed him up against the wall and he did not get scared, he kissed me back instead. Later that night we lost each other in the crowd when we were going to buy more beer, and I followed a classmate home instead and stayed over in his tiny student flat.

Two days later Johan was suddenly standing there on the train. It was not so late at night this time so I just said hello.

'Hi!' he said smiling wide, his eyes sparkling.

It turned out that he lived in Sandsborg too and we talked about the strange flat he and his friend were sub-letting, which looked like an old brothel. Creepy men rang the bell in the middle of the night and the furniture, which came with the flat, included beds covered in red velvet and paintings with erotic motifs.

I told him about my building where an old man often stood, pissing in the stairwell when I came home at night, holding his dick with one hand and waving at me with the other. Then the train stopped and we said *Goodbye, maybe we'll see each other around? Yes, maybe we will.*

And sometimes I really think the world is filled with magic, or is it fate? Because not a day passed without us running into each other again on the train. Either it was in the middle of the night on the way home from a bar, or early in the morning when I was on my way to a lecture at the university.

Finally I invited him over for red wine and quiche, and to my surprise and joy he just seemed happy and not scared. We talked and danced in my little studio flat and in the middle of the night we went downstairs to see if we could find the man pissing, but everything was quiet and dark so we went back to my bed and lay down like spoons and went to sleep. I woke up to find Johan looking at me with his beautiful, brown eyes and then I could not help but kiss him. He still did not get scared. After he left, I wrote in my journal that I would marry him, that if I was ever going to have children it would be with him.

The next day I woke up with a fever and Johan came by after work with mandarins, bottled water and chocolate. He crawled down next to me in bed and pulled the covers over us. We stayed in bed for three days and lived on mandarins and chocolate and hard bread. On the fourth day we were starving, so Johan went out and bought a roasted chicken and crisps which we quickly ate before jumping back under the covers.

That is more than ten years ago now. An eternity. I do not know who I was then and I am not sure I know who I am today. The greatest portion of my adult life has been spent with Johan. A life filled with dreams, longing, will, and disappointments, all so interconnected that I can no longer tell what is longing and what is disappointment. I just know that it is filled with shitty, emotional stains.

That is why I love reading about Isadora's confusion; then I do not feel so alone. Isadora hungers for and desires Adrian and does everything to make Bennett disappear. She makes sure she finds every opportunity to get together with Adrian while at the same time being filled with guilt about Bennett.

Perhaps if the zipless fuck actually worked, encounters which hurt no one; if you could speak openly about what you'd done, as friends. I know in any case that I have not stopped desiring other men even though I have loved Johan for more than ten years now. I know it is entirely possible to have all sorts of feelings for others, even if right here and now on Tenerife, I am just enjoying the solitude and the sleep. Isadora on the other hand, is burning with desire for sex.

> What was wrong with marriage anyway? Even if you loved your husband, there came that inevitable year when fucking him turned as bland as Velveeta cheese: filling, fattening even, but no thrill to the taste buds, no bittersweet edge, no danger. And you longed for an overripe Camembert, a rare goat cheese: luscious, creamy, cloven-hoofed.

But I do not think having sex with Johan is boring. It is not at all like a Velveeta cheese, more like aged cheddar, hard and dependable both for weekdays and special occasions. Cheese with a lot of flavour. A cheese that keeps at least ten years.

Once during secondary school, three of my best friends and I talked about what kind of cheese we would be if it could be translated into our personalities. Cissi became an aged Pastor's Cheese, because she was obsessed with studying theology at university at the time. Charlotte was brie, because sure enough, she became a legal expert and has the income and the taste for the more expensive types of cheese. I do not remember what kind of cheese Sanna became, but I remember my desperation when the others, without hesitation, agreed that I was a taco-flavoured cheese spread. The kind you can buy for twelve kronor at Ica.

So cheap! So American!

I was genuinely sad. My friends defended their decision by saying that I was flavoursome and if anyone liked those kinds of cheeses it was me. In any case, I have never really got over it. The others became wonderful aristocratic cheeses with centuries of heritage while I became a very typical working class cheese. A taco cheese.

As I am sitting in this café in Puerto de la Cruz thinking about cheese, I wish that I longed for adventure instead. Why am I thinking about cheese? Why do I get so upset about being propositioned by Danes?

Even my sex dreams are about Johan! I do not know if it is because I have a strong superego and so much guilt that I suppress all other kinds of desire, or if maybe it is just that I am completely fulfilled in my ten-year sex life with Johan

But Isadora's longing just burns more and more until finally she decides to follow her desire.

> I thought of all the cautious good-girl rules I had lived by – the good student, the dutiful daughter, the guilty, faithful wife who committed adultery only in her own head – and I decided that for once I was going to be brave and follow my feelings no matter what the consequences.

So beloved, confused Isadora leaves Bennett and heads off with Adrian in his car through Europe, and it does not take long before she realizes that she has made a huge mistake. While Isadora thought that they were driving aimlessly around Europe, it turns out that Adrian had his own private agenda: he has decided to meet up with his wife and children in Brittany, where they are going to have a two week holiday.

Suddenly Isadora finds herself alone in Paris without a lover or a husband to lean on. She sits there, just like me, alone in a café with a beer and tries to look indifferent. We are about the same age, both married, though Isadora does not have any children yet and is infinitely more tired than I am after her and Adrian's crazy road trip.

There at the café, Isadora suddenly realizes that what she did wrong.

> I had pursued him. Years of having fantasies about men and never acting on them – and then for the first time in my life, I live out a fantasy. I pursue a man I madly desire, and what happens? He goes limp as a waterlogged noodle and refuses me.

LIKE A WHORE

When you are so turned on you are about to explode it is easy to forget how taboo it is – if you are a woman that is, and you do not want to get the cold shoulder or be called a whore. It does not matter if you are thirty or thirteen.

But when I was thirteen nobody told me I was not allowed to be just as horny, relentless, and as willing as the boys, something I bitterly experienced one of the first times I was snogging someone. Fredrik L was a boy in my class and he froze out of fear and shock. We were lying on Cissi's bed, while she and Anders were on the black leather sofa in the living room. Bryan Adams was singing about Heaven and how fun the summer of '69 was and everything was perfect except for the fact that Fredrik had stopped stroking my back. He had actually stopped kissing me and was trying to sit up.

'Let's slow down a bit, OK?' I remember him saying.

I was horribly embarrassed because I suspected my persistent humping against his thigh had been a bit too much. But for just a few wonderful seconds I had shed all my inhibitions and felt only pure and simple desire. Time had stood still and I wanted to rub myself against him for all eternity.

Fredrik was considered good looking and I suppose he was the one who had taken the initiative, that he was used to being the one humping stiff, rigid female bodies and not, like now, being humped. Afterwards he spread a rumour that I was horny as a damned whore and for I long time I decided to be careful about ever being horny again.

That same summer I was called a whore for the second time in my life. We were camping with good friends of Mum and Dad's and their five children. It was the summer holidays and it was Öland and it was the sea and I felt grown up and relatively pretty. I had bought a new dress, it was sleeveless and tight and made from a black, shiny material. I remember wearing the dress almost every day.

One evening I went with Frank, the son of the friends who was the same as age as me, to buy some sweets at the only kiosk at the camp site, and he told me that his father had said at dinner that he thought I looked like a whore in that dress.

I do not know if I actually became sad, it was more that I thought it was disgusting of his father to look at me in that way. And I never wore that dress again.

The third time I was called a whore was in a hotel lift a year later. My boyfriend and I were there to meet his mother and we were sharing the lift with three men in their fifties in business suits. One of them looked at me for a while and said, 'And what's a whore like you doing tonight?'

I was so shocked I just politely replied, 'I'm going to be with my boyfriend.'

They thought it was hilarious and laughed the whole way up. My boyfriend did not say anything, but I saw his cheeks and neck turn blotchy. Then I became embarassed and wanted to apologize.

Since I turned thirteen, I have been called a whore about once a year by all kinds of men, in all possible and impossible situations: at the bar when I have not been in the mood to play along, or on the phone, when an anonymous man's voice has whispered 'Whore, whore, whore, whore.'

'OK,' I said.

Then he said it one more time, 'Whore, whore, whore, whore.' Only then did I hang up and I did not answer the phone again for the rest of the night.

There were so many tiny signs reprimanding my open horniness. It should never have reached the point at which someone called me a whore, subtler gestures would have sufficed. Like the time when a boy I'd met was going to come over for dinner.

I was single, enjoying having survived a boring relationship with a boring bloke and I was not the least bit interested in starting a new one. On the other hand, I definitely wanted several partners, preferably ones who would take over, one after the other.

This bloke was new and so far we had only kissed each other at a party, deep passionate kisses that promised more. Now, a night or so later, he was coming over for dinner and we could finally have sex.

It was wonderful and afterwards I lay in his arms, naked and satisfied. Then he suddenly asked if I had been offended that he had brought condoms with him. At first I did not understand. What did he mean? It was great. He looked a bit embarrassed and said that it could have seemed planned, like he had taken for granted that we would have sex. I understood that it was a well-mannered consideration, but I could not help noticing how shocked he was when he understood that I'd had the same thing in mind. That quite clearly didn't gel with his idea of who would be doing the conquering and who would be conquered. He never came back and I realized that I had broken some stupid unwritten rule yet again.

Young horny thirteen-year-old boys spreading rumours about their female classmates is not really all that strange when lawyers in business suits are calling rape victims whores during their testimony. The first time I interviewed this type of lawyer was when I was making a documentary about a gang rape in Södertälje. A girl thought she was getting a ride home from the bar, instead she was repeatedly raped by several different men, who simply drove her around during the night, raping her at different places: a school playground, a swimming pool, in a car park, in a flat. There were people present the whole time, while she was alone and drunk.

In the trial that followed, the court wasn't able to make up its mind. The Court of Appeal interpreted the law in such a way that she had been too drunk for it to be considered rape – in order for it to be deemed rape you have to have physically resisted and she obviously had not. But she was not drunk enough for it to be deemed sexual exploitation either, the milder form of sexual assault. Because, according to the Court of Appeal, she remembered too much of the events of the night, and in order for a case to be deemed sexual exploitation the victim needs to be completely impaired so as to be practically unconscious or otherwise powerless.

Despite the fact that she was alone and there were several suspects, the court did not regard her as powerless. Their ruling was just the opposite, that it was remarkable she had not tried to escape when she'd had so many opportunities to do so.

Björn was the first defence attorney I met, a man in his sixties with a large office on one of the main streets in

Södertälje, who loved to play golf. What Björn thought was most remarkable about the entire case was that the victim had a reputation as a whore.

'She said herself that when she moved to Sorunda she was singled out as a whore, and she doesn't know why. It's a bit strange if you move to a new neighbourhood and you become known as a whore without the residents even knowing you.'

'But in what way does this, in your opinion, have anything to do with her trustworthiness?' I asked.

'It diminishes her trustworthiness because if the rumour exists there must be some reason for it. That is to say, she previously had sexual relations, loose sexual relations.'

I did not really follow the reasoning and I was not prepared for this type of argument, so I pressed him to explain what he meant. Björn dug himself deeper into a hole filled with peculiar explanations and finally he described how drunk she was and that she was not particularly attractive – implying that she had been so flattered by the attention of these men that she had gone along with almost anything.

The other two defence attorneys, whom I met separately, also talked about how drunk she was and that she was rumoured to be a whore and that a rumour like that does not stem from nothing . . .

'She was no Greta Garbo,' one of them said.

I will never, ever forget their elegant suits, spacious offices or estimable ages. They will forever be etched in my memory. They represented the key to understanding what the concept of a whore is really about: power over our sexuality.

During the trial the lawyers successfully referred to her reputation as well as her 'ugliness' as a part of their clients' defence. The judge didn't interrupt them; the Swedish Bar

Association didn't suggest that there had been any injustice in her treatment. (I called the Legal Society and asked if lawyers could really say such things at trial, which they could, according to the chairwoman Anne Ramberg.)

A few years later at another rape trial, several women gathered to be present during the Court of Appeal proceedings. It turned out that in the district proceedings, everyone attending had been men, except the victim, Charlotte, and her plaintiff's assistant. As a result, the questions coming from the lawyers were insulting and to a large extent focused on her previous sexual experiences, her 'morals', and her drinking habits. So when the case went to the Court of Appeal we sat there, about twenty women, staring angrily at the lawyers as they cross examined the witness. Afterwards the plaintiff's assistant explained that there was an entirely different mood in the court room. The questions were quite simply more respectful and relevant.

Of course it is obvious that lawyers and judges are just as affected by each other's pats on the back as by the women's angry stares. At least it is clear to everyone else that the legal system and the law are in no way objective, nor created in a vacuum free from value judgments.

And I think that as long as we have a legal system that sanctions this archaic view of women, then we will also have young boys calling their classmates whores. And Isadora and the rest of us horny women will be met by limp, dangling spaghetti each time we have the desire to take the initiative.

EVERYTHING STINGS

I am thirteen and I have just realized that I am not so ugly after all. I am standing in front of the mirror at Cissi's house and she is standing next to me, we are looking at our reflections and feeling sorry for ourselves. The silent rule is that she says how ugly and fat she is, and I protest loudly and say that I'm the one who is hideous. Then Cissi screams, 'Nooo! You're not ugly!' And we stand there like that for an eternity, going around in circles.

But my secret, which I have never ever told Cissi, is that I no longer think I am that ugly. I feel a pleasant tingle in my stomach sometimes when I look at myself in the mirror, and I feel ashamed because I am supposed to despise myself as much as possible, anything else would be disgusting. So I continue to stand in front of the mirror with Cissi, pretending to cry and say, 'Why, why am I so damn, horribly ugly?'

And then Cissi really starts crying and says, 'If you think you're ugly, then you must think I'm grotesque!'

And then I have to protest again and say, 'That's not what I meant!' Then I cry even more and finally Cissi's mum knocks on the door and asks us what is going on.

We look at each other, our faces red and swollen from crying, and now we are almost ugly for real, so Cissi says 'Nothing! We're not doing anything!' We go out to the kitchen and make toast with thick layers of butter and marmalade, since we are so damn ugly and fat it does not matter any more. We might as well become even uglier and fatter with even more pimples.

We eagerly cultivate our self-contempt, and when others want to offer stupid comments we play along eagerly. Our maths and physics teacher introduces himself as Nils and says that he likes fishing and moose hunting. During our physics lesson he talks about his stupid wife who did not understand that she could not use her hairdryer in the hotel in Spain. There was a different voltage there, and even though he tried to explain the laws of physics to her she was stubborn. He asks if we know what happened. Henrik raises his hand and says that the hairdryer broke.

'That's absolutely right and it confirms something I've suspected for a long time, that women seem to have a harder time understanding maths and physics than men.'

The whole class laughs, even Cissi and me, and it seems as though Nils was right, because after a few weeks several of the girls are struggling to keep up with both maths and physics. I do not understand his lessons and our first physics test provides the proof, I only get three out of twenty-five answers right.

Nils likes to talk during class, especially about his moose hunting, and we listen attentively and ask lots of questions, because it is a lot more fun listening to his encounters with moose than learning maths.

'Please Nils, show us how you lured the moose bull by sounding like a female,' I ask, and Nils happily puts his hands to his mouth and pounds out a trumpeting bellow.

When everyone laughs Nils seems to wake up from his day-dream and he immediately becomes serious and looks at the clock.

'Well, class is over for today. Sara, would you stay behind a minute so I can speak to you?'

I give Cissi a questioning look and she whispers that she will wait outside.

Nils walks over and sits down on the edge of my desk.

'Well Sara, I've noticed that you aren't very interested in either maths or physics.'

'Nope, not really.' I squirm in my chair.

'No, and it was also clear from the physics test, in which you got a terrible mark. I won't tolerate you disrupting the class by asking a lot of nonsense about my moose hunting, so that's why I want to suggest an agreement.'

'OK?'

'If you sit quietly and leaf through *Illustrated Science* I will give you a pass regardless of how well you do in the exams.'

I look at him in surprise and quickly try and consult with myself. I had not realized I was disrupting the class, but I know that I am stupid and Nils thinks so too and it does not matter how hard I study.

'OK,' I say, embarrassed.

Nils smiles and pats me on the shoulder.

'Good, then we're agreed. You're an attractive girl Sara, you don't need to know maths or physics!'

'OK,' I say curtly, and I go to meet Cissi who is waiting outside.

Something has happened, something has changed, and I feel it and Cissi feels it and one day when we are standing outside the mall Stefan comes walking towards us. He is twenty-two years old and has curly dark hair and black, skinny jeans. He is so grown up and so damned good-looking and now he is walking this way. I have seen him in the city several times and longed for someone like him and now he is coming over. He is actually walking straight towards us, and he is looking at us. He looks at me and smiles and I smile back and I am frozen on the spot because I know that if I move now I am going to start shaking uncontrollably.

'Hi!' he says, and looks me right in the eye.

'Hi!' I say, and look back.

'I've seen you around town. My name is Stefan, what's yours?'

'Sara,' I say and try and understand what he is saying, that he has seen me. Where has he seen me? In the city?

'Do you want to come over to my place for a cup of coffee? I live right behind the mall.'

I look at him and then at Cissi who is staring at the ground, embarrassed, and I feverishly try to work out how I should act, and then I decide I do not have the energy to care any more. This is a new game, different from our usual ugliness contest and I do not know which rules apply now. A warm tingle overpowers me and spreads from my legs to my pelvis, up through my stomach and finally reaches my mouth which, I realize in panic, has broken into a wide, open smile directed at Stefan. He grins back and holds out his hand, I take it and I follow him. I turn around and say bye to Cissi who has stopped staring at the ground and is now watching us.

We walk hand in hand, grinning, back to his place. His hand is warm and every now and then he squeezes mine and looks at me with his nice, brown eyes which are glittering.

He stops outside his building, pulls me towards him and kisses me. A deep, intense kiss that makes everything spin and pound. If he only knew – how amazing my dreams have been, how I've longed to be worshipped, how I've hungered for closeness! If he suspected my starvation, my hunger, he would never dare touch me in this way. But he does not know and I push myself against him hard and I can feel myself becoming damp and swollen.

He lives in a small studio flat with a kitchenette; there are IKEA shelves filled with LPs, a bed and a small coffee table. He offers me coffee and cinnamon rolls his mother has baked and he tells me that he always eats cinnamon rolls for breakfast. I think that is why his breath is so bad, a small detail I am happy to ignore when my body feels happy and feverish.

We kiss each other on his unmade bed and he caresses my small breasts and it feels good. I am lying with my arms stretched above my head, my eyes are closed and I am just enjoying. I let the hours pass while I become even sweatier. His stubble scratches me and when we take a short break I look in the mirror and see that my lips and cheeks are scratched and red.

Stefan stands by the shelves and shows me his LPs and talks about different albums which are particularly valuable, and I smile wide and say uh-huh and we have nothing, absolutely nothing to talk about so we continue to kiss instead.

Suddenly it is evening, late at night, and I feel defiant when I think about how Mum and Dad are probably worried and wondering where I am, a pure and clean malicious pleasure. They can go ahead and wonder, I think to myself and I decide to stay the night. Something has grown inside me, a feeling of wanting to challenge and let things happen, a feeling of letting go.

We are lying on his unmade bed. He unbuttons his trousers, takes my hand and puts it on his penis and I touch it like I think you are supposed to. I am not entirely sure because I have only touched one cock before in my fourteen years. The first time was when I was thirteen and I was with a boy from my year and I just squeezed it. I had read a sex scene in a Stephen King novel in which the wife of the main character walks over to him while he is in the bath and squeezes his dick. It sounded exciting and it was the only information I had about how the male anatomy works. So I squeezed and squeezed until the poor fellow told me to pull up and down instead.

This time with Stefan I know what a foreskin is and I know that you are supposed to move up and down. He comes on my hand and it is warm and slimy. He kisses my forehead and I go and get some toilet paper so we can wipe ourselves off. We still have nothing, absolutely nothing to talk about, so we kiss some more. My body is not quite as sweaty and feverish as it was earlier, it is not pounding everywhere and maybe it is almost, but only almost, beginning to get boring? I see that it is past midnight and I wonder if we are going to fall asleep because suddenly I am exhausted, but Stefan seems to have other ideas. His breathing is heavy and his fingers are searching my body, inside nooks which are previously untouched. It feels strange and unfamiliar and I try and push his hand away, because now it is moving hard, bumping inside me. It is pinching and groping, like an instrument made of stainless steel. It is not a warm hand any longer. I try and look into his beautiful brown eyes, but he closes them and is unreachable. Something is cold, I think it is me and I try and change position but Stefan is pinning my arms and lying down on top of me and I am having a hard time breathing. He fumbles with his trousers and

I can feel how his hardness is trying to find its way between my legs, which are pressed together. I try to resist, but Stefan is much stronger and slowly my legs are pushed apart.

Just then, when I think I am going to suffocate because I cannot get any more air, just then, when I really start to panic, the doorbell rings. Stefan freezes, opens his eyes and looks at me. He seems surprised and I realize that my face is wet. I must have been crying. I wipe the tears away with the back of my hand and Stefan still looks half asleep when he leaves the room to open the door. Dad is standing there and he looks serious.

'You have five minutes to get to the car, where I'll be waiting,' he says, turns around and leaves. I blush with shame from being exposed as the fourteen year old I am, and I can see from Stefan's red face that he is embarrassed too. I gather my clothes, my school bag and carefully tie my Doc Martens' boots while Stefan sits on the edge of the bed watching me.

Everything is quiet, there is a swishing sound in my head and the only thing I can think about is how many LPs he has. So many, an amazing number.

Dad is silent in the car on the way home, but it is not a punishing silence and I am grateful that he is not yelling at me. I stare straight ahead at the road and see the headlights making yellow tracks in the black night.

My brain slowly starts working again, and I wonder how much Dad knows, what he saw. But I do not say anything, I do not dare explain or ask because it feels like my cheeks are red with shame, red from tears and hard kisses.

But later, when I am lying in my own bed, in my own room, in my own body, in our quietly sleeping terrace house, it comes. The fear. An abyss with steep sides that drop straight down. I lie stretched out under the covers, staring out into the darkness for what feels like an eternity, until I hear Mum get up and set out breakfast.

I go to school as usual and when Cissi asks me what it was like and if I am in love I say yes, maybe a little. But he is so much older, and since I am so ugly he is never going to want to go out with me.

When Stefan calls the next evening and says hi, I say hi back. He is quiet for a while and so am I, but finally he says that he does not think it is going to work between us. OK, I say. Bye. Bye, he says.

The next evening when I am on my way home from Cissi's it happens again, a black abyss which overwhelms me. It is autumn and the evenings have just started to grow cold and dark. I am biking home the usual way between the houses and the streets are quiet and empty. Suddenly I hear a car driving slowly behind me. My head starts spinning and at first I do not dare turn around and look, I just listen to how it is creeping along, following me. I bike faster and I hear it speed up. I can feel the heat from the headlights which are close to my legs. My head is pounding and when I see the playground in front of me I turn off the road and bike as quickly as I can between the swings, the sandpits and the jungle gyms. The car is forced to drive along the road, to the side. There is a phone box in the playground and I stop there but my hands are shaking so much I cannot get the coin in the slot. I finally manage and I dial home where I know Dad will be sitting on the leather couch with his cocktail.

'Dad!' I cry. 'Dad! There's a car following me!'

'What? Where are you?' he replies, and when I hear that he is anxious it frightens me even more and I am crying so hard I can barely talk.

'Sara!' I hear him yell on the other end of the line, 'you have to tell me where you are!'

'In the park,' I cry between sobs. 'I'm in the park and he is somewhere here too!'

'Stay where you are, I'm on my way! Do you hear me Sara?'

'Yes,' I sob, 'hurry!'

I stand there and do not dare look because I know that the phone box is lit and the park is pitch black and he might show up at any moment, the unknown driver, the man without a face. But nothing happens and finally Dad comes, he tears open the door to the phone box and gives me a long, hard hug. He puts my bike in the boot and when we are sitting in the car I can see that his hands are shaking too.

'Did you get the licence plate number?' he asks.

'No, I was afraid to look. I just biked,' I answer.

'How can you be so stupid?' he asks angrily. 'Don't you understand that we need the licence plate number in order to catch him?'

I start crying again and try and explain that I was so scared I didn't think of it. Dad grunts and yells the whole way home, mumbling about stupid women and idiots and I stare out into the pitch black night one more time and think about how lucky I am that I did not tell him about Stefan. What damn good luck that I have not said anything to anyone.

How could I ever explain my excitement, the way everything was spinning and pounding and how it suddenly wasn't there any longer? That it was over and his fingers became hard?

It is autumn and I am cold all the time and each day after school I crawl under the covers to get warm. I lie there and fantasize about a grown-up life in New York, about men in business suits who have money and want to take me out. They love me and I love them, I make love to all of them, one after another. It makes them grateful and happy and they say that they have never met anyone like me, *ever*. I am fourteen and I cannot stop hungering even though I suspect that it is hurting me. I want so badly and so eagerly. Most of all I want to be grown up and worshipped.

One day on the bus it happens, a daydream that almost becomes reality. I have forgotten my bus pass and I am trying to convince the driver that I am just fourteen so I should pay the youth price. The driver smiles at me and says that it should be a crime to be fourteen and so beautiful. He introduces himself and tells me his name is Jens and he is twenty-one.

And I smile like an idiot and feel the tingling happiness in my chest make everything grow warm, and two hours later we are sitting across from each other drinking coffee at Hallström's Café.

This time I do not make the same mistake as I did with Stefan, although I almost do. It takes a while before we go to his place. For months we take endless walks, watch a hundred movies at the cinema and spend hours in my room with Mum and Dad at a safe distance in the kitchen. But it is all a matter of time, because I am constantly hungering to be grown up for real and I know what I need to do to seal our contract of love, my contract of adulthood.

One night we decide it is time and shortly thereafter Jens forces himself into my dry, narrow fourteen-year-old cunt which actually does not want his dick, but something else. It burns and hurts and a red blood-stain stares angrily up at us from the white sheet. But everything is real now and I stay at Jens's place almost every night. I have a toothbrush and a pair of underwear in my school bag, together with my books, pens and lip balm.

Jens is nice and he thinks that he loves me and I think that I love him. We listen to Sinead O'Connor and assure each other that nothing, absolutely nothing compares to you!

He whispers things in my ear when we make love, beautiful things I like to hear. His words make me forget that my cunt is dry and I walk around with a constant burning sensation. It takes a month before we realize that he has given me chlamydia and herpes. He gets his test results over the phone and I see his face turn red.

'It must be from backpacking last summer,' he says, embarrassed.

Doubled over I limp to the bathroom, because hot baths are the only thing that help ease the pain for a time. Mum wonders why my stomach hurts and I say that I do not know. When she tells me to make an appointment with the gynaecologist I do not protest. The receptionist who answers is kind and understanding and she makes the appointment for the following week. I do not protest either when Mum wants to come with me. I have never been to a gynaecologist before, but I suspect that it will be disgusting and unpleasant.

Mum waits outside while I go into the examination room. The male gynaecologist is waiting, sitting with his back towards me, but spins his chair around when he hears me open the door. He smiles wide and I stare in surprise when I realize that it is our neighbour.

Then I am lying in the chair with my legs spread, being examined by Per-Ove who lives in a yellow house in our street. I usually wave when I cycle past. Per-Ove works in his garden a lot.

'Well,' says Per-Ove, pulling on his rubber gloves, and sitting down to look between my legs.

'How are Mum and Dad?'

'Good I think.' I answer quietly because suddenly I have run out of air and my throat feels constricted.

'Well, good,' says Per-Ove and pushes something that looks like a cake cutter made of stainless steel inside me.

'Have you got any apples on the trees yet?'

'Don't know,' I reply shortly, because it is burning like fire between my legs and I need to concentrate so I will not scream.

'Our apples were also late this year,' Per-Ove says, and pulls out the tongs, hard and quick.

'Ow!' I sob and I start to cry.

'There now, that wasn't so bad!' Per-Ove says, and pushes in a cotton bud. 'That's what happens when you're out and about not being careful!' he says, and smiles crookedly.

I look at his eyes which are staring at my insides. Small, narrow pig-like eyes embedded in thick, fat wrinkles. Shiny beads of sweat are forming on the top of his bald head. I look at the black pores which discolour his vein-covered nose. Having his nose down there, far too close, feels more degrading than anything else.

'Yes, it definitely looks like herpes. We will find out about the chlamydia in a few days, but you can count on having that as well since your boyfriend is infected,' he says, and takes off the gloves and throws them in the bin.

He grins widely and watches me openly while I clumsily get down from the chair. I am shaking as I try and put on my underwear because Per-Ove is still staring at me. He has sat down at his desk now and is leaning back with his hands crossed over his enormous stomach. He is sitting quietly, grinning the whole time I am getting dressed, and I feel a fury grow beneath my embarrassment. It pulls and tears and when I turn around in the doorway, I hate. I stare right back into Per-Ove's scornful eyes and see his grinning mouth and yes, I really hate him. I want to say something, maybe hurt him, because I am tired of being fourteen, tired of constantly being controlled by boyfriends, faceless men, Mum and Dad.

But most of all I want to get Per-Ove to stop smiling that ugly, fat grin of his.

'Don't look so satisfied!' I say as I stare back. 'Don't you know that everyone thinks male gynaecologists are disgusting?'

Per-Ove stiffens, his eyes grow wide for a brief second and he opens his mouth to say something, but I beat him to it.

'Damn sadistic pervert!' I hiss and walk out, slamming the door hard behind me.

In the waiting room I see Mum get up from the sofa and my anger quickly disappears and is replaced by deep embarrassment.

'What did he say?' she asks when we have left the waiting room.

'That I have chlamydia and herpes,' I reply.

She does not say anything, just continues walking along the long hospital corridor, looking straight ahead. We walk like this, quietly, side by side, all the way to the lift at the end. She is going back to work and I am going to school. The lift comes and I get in, but when I turn around I see that she has not followed me. She is still standing in the hospital corridor outside and looks me in the eye for the first time.

'You should be ashamed,' she says as the lift door closes. Her lips are narrow and I see that they are trembling with anger.

I look at the closed lift door in surprise and think how

strange it is that she hasn't understood – that the only feeling in my entire body is shame, nothing but shame. Did she think I was proud?

And I can never explain that the only thing I have done is try to survive. Escaping to Jens was an alternative, the only one then, and this time there was not a parent stopping me. Having sex with Jens burned and made me sore but it was still better than having to be around Mum and Dad's humiliation; the only way to avoid being infected by their anxiety.

That is the way it was, even if I wish there had been another way to grow up than through these voluntary rapes. Maybe if I had been drunk. Or a boy.

PEACOCK

If I ever have a daughter I hope she will not be pretty. Being a pretty girl turns you into prey, an easy victim for shitty, sexist socialization. The kind of socialization that leads girls to think their worth lies in their appearance. If you are not all that pretty then there is a chance you will make it by fostering some sort of talent, like being good at school.

Being fourteen and pretty, combined with an insatiable need for acknowledgement, was devastating for me. It is just pure and simple luck that things did not turn out any worse than they did. At one point I shaved off my hair and I have never been as ugly or as free, but then I started longing to be pretty again. That is how it rears its ugly head, the need to flirt.

Feeling invisible can create such a exhausting hunger you will do almost anything, even if to some extent there was a kind of freedom in my parents' lack of interest. Sometimes I am grateful they never asked if I had done my homework, how the test went, or what I was drawing or thinking. For some of my friends who grew up in upper-middle-class homes, these parental demands created a huge amount of anxiety and feelings of inadequacy.

But maybe it remains easier if those demands come from your parents rather than from yourself. In the best case scenario you can rebel against your parents, and I think that is simpler than rebelling against yourself.

My own need for acknowledgement has never really disappeared, it has just taken on new forms. When I started having obsessive thoughts about being a peacock, I realized that work was not all it was cracked up to be. For a long time the only thing I felt good at was being a journalist, even though I despise the myth of the artist, which assumes that certain people are simply born with talent, something you either do or do not have. And it just so happens that the ones who are seen as being talented are often white men from the middle classes, at least according to the those who have the power to define what an artist is and create space for them.

I hated the speeches made by the director of the University College of Film, Radio, Television and Theatre at the end of each term. It was always about how some of us were talented artists and others not. So naïve, so middle class, elitist and grandfather-like! Despite this my desire grew and at university I felt recognized and acknowledged for the first time in my life.

When I started working at Swedish Radio, the silence came as a shock. It was a silence that was deafening, weighed down by meanness and it crushed my fragile longing to be seen. I remember how surprised I was when my first documentary aired and no one said anything, neither management nor colleagues. I thought the world would end. It took several years before I realized that it had nothing to do with me, my potential talent or worth; it was simply the ruling culture.

The image of the peacock started to pop up in my head just after I won an award for a documentary. Up until that moment, a prize like that had been the best thing I could have imagined when it came to being acknowledged. The strange thing was that once it happened, I did not feel anything. I was barely happy, and suddenly images of peacocks popped into my head when I was biking, shopping or picking up Sigge from daycare. I would be standing in front of the mirror, tying a yellow ribbon in my hair and I would see a peacock.

The emptiness of it all was suddenly so visible, just as it had been when I was getting married and it was all great fun until it was time to stand up before all of the guests. Then I realized to what extent a wedding was just a display, a performance in which we would be shown off and inspected. Then like now, I was embarrassed and I felt vain and silly and resentful. Why did I need to win awards? (Why did I need to get married?) What kind of crap is this? Competing in radio!

Then I found myself sitting with therapist Niklas yet again, crying because I was a damn peacock.

Why do unhappy people keep living together, year after year?

I think about this as I eat breakfast, watching all the couples. Sitting in the breakfast room with everyone disposes me to bitter bitchy thoughts, not because I have the slightest idea what their marriages are like, but when I amuse myself by trying to decide if any of the couples are happy, they all look resolute and embarrassed and it seems that this must mean something, that a suppressed silence is ruling in here.

I see one man gesticulating wildly with his arms while he explains something to his wife. At least they look like they are having some fun together, the look she is giving him is open. The women here in the breakfast room are all sitting, facing the men, with their bodies and their eyes. The men sit a bit turned away or they look straight ahead. Up until now I have not seen a single instance in which the man has been sitting, facing his wife. Even when they are sitting across from each other, the husband's eyes are staring off towards the horizon while the wife's are attentively focused on his, constantly ready to smile or parry.

The ones who look the happiest are two middle-aged women sitting at a table with flowers and candles. I caught sight of them when I heard a champagne bottle being opened by the waiter. Apparently one of them has her birthday today. That sort of thing makes me feel warm all over, it is so damn beautiful. I see them clink glasses, and their faces are very red. Maybe they feel a bit like outsiders in this couple-filled ghetto? Aside from them I'm completely surrounded by couples, couples, couples and then a few young families.

Maybe they're widows? Or divorced, since they are here without men (they looked a bit too ordinary to be lesbians, but then again that is just one of my countless prejudices). If you are a middle-aged woman you simply do not travel without your significant other, if you have one. At least it is very rare. And that goes for me, too. Men travel alone all over the world without anyone raising an eyebrow, but when women, regardless of age, do the same, people wonder what is wrong.

When I leave the breakfast room I see the happily gesticulating man. He is standing down by the cliff with his wife, looking at the ocean. He is still gesticulating wildly, as if he really has something to say, which maybe he does. But even if that is not the case I love him for trying. She looks happy and not as woeful as the rest of the wives here at La Quinta Park. The fact is that when I look around among the couples here at the hotel, the women are the ones doing the talking. Even the woeful ones are trying to carry on some sort of conversation.

I wonder what all of these quiet men are thinking. There is almost nothing that infuriates me so much as quiet men. A strange contrast to how loud men often are in other situations. So why do they often grow quiet in relationships? Nothing scares me more than Johan when he becomes quiet and distant.

There is a physical memory which makes me depressed and makes my knees and elbows itch like eczema. I am seven years old, and weighed down with Mum and Dad's silence; a silence containing everything, it is threatening and filled with failed encounters. *An organized form of an unlived life.*

This physical memory has left me overly sensitive to the silence between people. People who are quiet make me uncertain and fill me with contempt. I immediately write them off as mean. When Isadora travels with Bennett to Paris for their first Christmas as newlyweds, he suddenly becomes quiet.

> Throughout the whole long drive from Heidelberg to Paris, Bennett said almost not a word to me. Silence is the bluntest of blunt instruments. It seems to hammer you into the ground. It drives you deeper and deeper into your own guilt. It makes the voices inside your head accuse you more viciously than any external voices ever could.

I know exactly what you mean, Isadora. I wish I was there as a witness, a friend who could remind you that you have not done anything to deserve his punishing silence. A friend would say, 'Let's dump this quiet weirdo. He can stay here in the hotel room and sulk. Let's go and drink some fantastic French red wine instead!'

But I was not there in the hotel room in Paris, and Isadora becomes more and more desperate. After hours of silence she asks him what she has done and Bennett just asks her to forget about it.

'Forget what?' Isadora asks in a shrill voice, and Bennett says he does not want her screaming like that.

'I don't give a fuck what you won't have me do. I'd like to be treated civilly. I'd like you to at least do me the courtesy of telling me why you're in such a funk. And don't look at me that way . . .'

'What way?'

'As if my not being able to read your mind were my greatest sin. I *can't* read your mind. I *don't* know why you're so mad. I *can't* intuit your every wish. If that's what you want in a wife you don't have it in me.'

'I certainly don't.'

'Then what is it? Please tell me.'

'I shouldn't have to.'

'Good God! Do you mean to tell me I'm expected to be a mind reader? Is that the kind of mothering you want?'

And it continues like that. Isadora masturbates and cries herself to sleep while Bennett sleeps with his back to her. And I wish Isadora could call me so I could tell her what I read in Carin Holmberg's book *It's Called Love*. Carin Holmberg writes about a concept she calls 'Micro-power'. The lack of response, she says, is one of the ultimate expressions of a man's power. By the man not answering, the woman is forced into subordination and becomes a non-person. Being silent is a way of distancing yourself, it forces women to take over roles in order to understand the man's emotional mood and problems. This means that she actively relates to him while he does not relate to her to the same degree.

When I read this the for first time I cried because I was so affected by the clear-sightedness of Carin Holmberg's analysis.

'Damn autist!' I hissed at Johan once, after I had asked the same question three times without getting an answer. We had been out shopping and now he was standing there, contemplating the receipt.

'Do you know what happened to the spinach?' I asked.

No reply.

'Johan! Do you know what happened to the spinach?' I asked again.

He just continued to stare at the receipt, without replying or even looking up at me.

'DO YOU KNOW WHERE THE SPINACH IS!' I screamed far too loudly and hysterically. The cashier gave me a questioning look but now Johan finally looked up from his receipt.

'Don't yell! Can't you see I'm checking the receipt?' he said, irritated.

'Damn autist!' I said angrily and walked off, leaving him with all of the shopping bags and the receipt.

Do I exist? I thought as I walked towards the car and the humiliation intensified. Because I know that if he had asked a question, regardless of how busy I had been with the receipt, Sigge, a book, the TV or whatever, I would have answered. Always ready! Always ready to converse if an uncomfortable silence develops. I hate silence, because it could mean that we really are unhappy.

When Johan disappears into his quiet disconnectedness and

I ask what is going on, he always says that it is nothing. He does not reply with any cryptic insinuations that I ought to know, like Bennett. But the strange thing is despite the fact that he assures me it is nothing, absolutely nothing, his sulky silence tells a different story. The tiniest hesitation presents itself, and is impossible to ignore.

Sometimes I try to do the same thing, delay my answers a few seconds, just long enough to make him uncertain, force him to repeat the question while I continue with what I was doing as if I was so busy I hadn't heard. It is interesting to see that he reacts with the same uncertainty I do. It is interesting to experience the secure peace I then feel inside.

His silence is often worse in the morning. The silence, he says, comes from his tiredness and not being a morning person; that he has never been cheery in the morning. For a long time I accepted that as an explanation until I realized that his silence, if anything, was related to his good sleep and my ear plugs. I have always been impressed and jealous of Johan because he sleeps so well. He can fall asleep even in a bright room with the radio on. It does not bother him.

It is an ability he has, to shut out his surroundings.

When Sigge was born, I was infuriated when he asked how the night had been. Had he not noticed that I had got up five times to change nappies and feed Sigge? That my longest nap had been two hours? When it was Johan's turn to take Sigge one night, I woke up every time he got up. Sigge's whimpering often woke me first, and I had to wake up Johan so he would go to Sigge.

That is what life was like until it was enriched by two wonderful little pieces of rubber called ear plugs. A friend with the same experience had given me the tip about the ear plugs and suddenly everything was quiet. I could put in the ear plugs and say goodnight to Johan and let the wonderful silence take over. It was a way of handing over all the responsibility. Suddenly I was sleeping through the night and not waking up a single time when Johan got up to go to Sigge.

The nights when it was my turn to take Sigge remained sleepless, but at least now I got to sleep every other night. Now I was the one who cheerfully asked Johan how the night had been and Johan who, irritated, told me that he had been up every other hour between twelve and six.

Ear plugs must be God's gift to women. Sometimes, on certain mornings when Johan seems particularly distant, I have left the ear plugs in during breakfast and allowed myself to live in my own wonderfully quiet world while I read the newspaper and slowly let the coffee bring me to life. I have lost myself in an article and not reacted to Sigge's cries so god damned immediately. I have drunk my coffee slowly and stared listlessly at Johan's lips which moved when he said something to me.

'What?' I've asked. 'What did you say?'

I left the ear plugs in and made myself just as distant and silent as him, until he asked, frustrated, what was going on.

'Nothing. It's nothing I promise,' I replied, and continued reading the newspaper.

It is a way of achieving balance: he blames it on his bad mood in the morning, I blame it on the ear plugs. Sometimes I think the only way of achieving balance is to assimilate the behaviour and manners of men. It is not fun, but maybe it is a necessary evil. Women must let go of the responsibility, allow themselves to become just as sloppy, forgetful and selfish as their husbands.

Every time I take the train or the bus from work I hear at

least one mobile phone call from some man calling home to ask what he should buy at the shops.

'Hi sweetheart! Can you ask Mummy what kind of fish I needed to buy . . . Yes, OK, can you ask if there was anything else we needed?'

She is his private, comfortable computer memory. She is the one who needs to create space in her brain to make room for what food needs to be bought. Room she could have used for significantly more important and interesting thoughts than what kind of fish he needs to buy. She stores it in a safe place so that he just needs to call home when it is time for the information to be delivered.

I have never heard a woman call home to ask her husband the same thing, and I think about what will happen the day her hard drive becomes full, when it crashes. A small daydream about the day she suddenly starts replying with incomprehensible oddities.

'We need chocolate with a high percentage of cacao, red wine and more love, more tenderness, more time for each other and by the way I would really like to go to a tango course with you tonight!'

Or the day she just giggles and says that she does not have a fucking clue what they need to buy.

ORANGE MEN

I wake up in the middle of the night because I am freezing cold, and I have just had a very strange dream. I dreamed that my grandmother was going to kill me at eight p.m. She announced it during the afternoon in a threatening, agitated voice and I knew she meant it and I was frightened, despite her fragility. I had disappointed her in some way, so many times that enough was enough. I went home (in my dreams Mum and Dad are almost always still together) and told them about Grandma's death threat.

'Oh my,' Mum says anxiously.

Dad lights a cigarette and walks into another room with a resolute expression on his face. Then nothing happens for several hours.

'But don't you understand?' I say desperately. 'She's coming here at eight to kill me!'

'It's a shame she got so angry,' Mum says, while she continues doing the dishes in the kitchen. Dad still isn't saying anything; he goes out to the garage instead and closes the door.

When it is five minutes to eight I realize that if I want to survive I will have to take matters into my own hands. Grandma could be here at any moment. I quickly stuff some clothes in a bag and run to Mum, crying.

'I'm going to have to go away for a while, since you apparently aren't going to help me!' I say accusingly, feeling small and abandoned.

'Yes, maybe that's for the best,' Mum says indifferently, hugging me goodbye.

Dad was still in the garage when I left the house running, and jumped on the bus.

Now I am lying here in bed thinking that it is true. They could never protect me, and the dream recalled a familiar feeling of being alone and exposed. There was always a yearning, always depression. To think that secondary school graduation was one of the happiest days of my life – the day when I could really leave, walk away from the insecurity and all of the crap, the ugly wallpaper, the worn leather sofa, and the dust-filled carpet which made my eyes red and itchy. The day I finally became free from my family.

I walk out on to the balcony and watch the sun rise over the ocean. I feel the warmth in the air even though it is only six-thirty in the morning. To think that life can be like this, so fantastically beautiful and sad and horrible and completely good. I sit and look out over the ocean and the sun until breakfast is served.

I fill my plate with fresh watermelon, pour honey over the fat, tasty yoghurt, pick out two, newly baked rolls and top them with salty, smoked ham. I also take hot, black coffee and sweet orange juice. The sadness slowly lets go and I become happy again, mainly because of the watermelon. It makes me genuinely happy. I do not think you can feel anxious if you get to eat fresh watermelon for breakfast every day.

Later I lie down in a deck chair by the pool and read. A young English family is lying next to me. The parents are about my age and they have a little boy and a little girl. They are chatting while the children are playing by the edge of the pool and I get a stab of longing for Sigge, but then something happens. The little boy named George wants to run around the deep end of the pool. Dad sees this and yells: 'Come here Georgie! Georgie! GEORGIE! I'll count to three: One! Two! Three! . . . Well done! Good boy!'

Mum is drying off the little girl Jessica, and she wants to read her a story, but Jessica would rather run around the pool with her brother. I see the mum pull her daughter towards her and hold her on her lap.

'The Pink Princess. The Pink Princess was always dressed in pink. One day when she walked into the forest . . .' Suddenly she stops reading.

'Jessie! What have you done? You broke Mummy's sunglasses! Oh why, Jessie? Why!'

Their voices can be heard over the entire pool area, but you still have to admire their open frustration. No family shame here, no sir. The dad takes big steps over to the oh-ing mum.

'Look what she did! She broke my sunglasses!' she says to her husband, hurt.

I try to ignore the incestuous tone – she is talking like she is a little girl and not an equal partner. But her husband takes over his practised role as the all-powerful father.

'Jessie! Why are you ignoring Mummy! Say you're sorry!'

I stop listening at this point and go to the loo instead. When I come back it is calm for the time being and I can hear the mother explaining to little Georgie that 'Tomorrow we're going back to England.'

But there are exceptions to nuclear family hell. A Finnish family that came today looks really nice and happy. The father, dressed in a black T-shirt and beige shorts, rushed around getting deck chairs for everyone so that they could lie next to each other and sunbathe. When everyone in the family was settled, he stood a few feet away and got his digital camera out from his light-blue waist bag. He looked so proud as he took a picture of his family. I bet you he is the kind that peels oranges for his children. And his wife.

Men who peel oranges in public are extremely rare. So are men who bring a packed lunch to work. I love men who peel oranges. There is a kind of beautiful precision, a patience and a care in the peeling. A way of showing love in little ways; a desire to give without necessarily wanting something in return, because the only thing you get back is juice on your hands. It is a true act of love without prestige, which goes against so much in the male role.

And I love men who bring their lunch to work for the same reason, or bike or walk to work instead of taking the car. And men who dance. Why is there such a shortage of men who are willing to dance? Do not they understand that it is a perfect, awe-inspiring action, which shows they are humans who aren't afraid to reveal themselves? Instead, little boys are taught to be afraid of expressing themselves physically in the open, sensitive way that is part of dancing. In contrast to sports, dancing is not about competing and winning. These boys become men who stand there on the side with their beer, staring stupidly at all the girls who are dancing with each other, and looking like they need to take a shit. This is one of my few requirements: no more men who do not want to dance!

The Finnish family dad stands protectively behind his

sunbathing family and looks at them proudly. Definitely an orange man!

And he takes pictures of them. One of my friends told me that she had grown up thinking she was Daddy's little girl, not because she had many memories of her dad taking part in family activities, he was usually away on business, but because the family album was stuffed with photos of her and her father. There were only a few pictures of her and her mother, and that is why she assumed Dad had been around more than she remembered. Until one day she realized that the person who had taken all of the pictures of her and her father was her mother. She was the kind of woman who is constantly covering up the absence of her husband, creating stories and pictures to lessen the child's longing. Maybe that is why fathers have such a predominant role in children's books and films.

One of Sigge's favourite films is *Finding Nemo*, in which a father fish spends the entire film searching for his son who has been taken away to an aquarium. The mother is quite simply dead, like Pippi Longstocking's mother. And where is Alfons Åberg's mother? No one knows.

It is as if stories for children have also been forced to compensate for the father's absence in real life.

I know a lot of people who have grown up without their fathers, but no one who has grown up without a mother. I know a few whose fathers have actually been present. Dads who have shared custody, and dads who have not worked and worked and worked. But there are not many. There are far fewer of them than all of the fathers I know who have never been around, who have just come home and played a guest role on the weekends. Fathers who have cooked fancy dinners on Fridays and Saturdays before it was time to leave again on Monday morning.

I suppose it must feel good to be missed so; so wonderful in fact that you might misunderstand the whole thing and become proud and fulfilled or write a song about your daughter's loss? *Dad come home. Because I miss you. Come before the summer is over, Dad.*

And then everybody thinks it is sweet when it is actually horribly sad.

There is one stuffy June morning I will never forget. The liver pâté was mouldy, which is the most disgusting thing I know, and Johan had been away working for several weeks and home only at the weekends. Sigge missed him and I missed him and we were walking through the park on our way to daycare, two tired and sad souls. Sigge was sitting quietly in the buggy. He usually asks about everything we see along the way, why the air is so transparent, where the sun actually lives and if I like ice cream with pears and whipped cream. But today he was just sitting there quiet and tired, and I wanted to stop and hold him but instead I walked even faster. And then in the middle of the silence his questions started to come.

'Mommy, why does Daddy have to work in Växjö?'

I gave him a tired, noncommittal answer.

'He just has to. That's where his job is right now.'

'But why?' Sigge continued.

'To earn money so we can buy food and pay the rent.'

'Why?' Sigge said again, and I realized that he really did not understand and then I started wondering whether *I* really understood.

'People have to work,' I said and heard how hollow it sounded.

'Why?' said Sigge, and I realized that I really did not have a good answer. It became even clearer to me that no one forces us; these are personal, independent choices. But I could not tell Sigge that. I could not tell Sigge that Johan really wanted to work in Växjö. It is hopeless thinking that there always seem to be a thousand legitimate reasons for making unequal choices. *We need the money*. Nope, we actually do not, we have enough to get by. But we need each other and your child needs you!

I am also one of those mothers taking pictures of their child with his father in order to compensate for his absence. For lack of a harmonious present you must create a harmonious past.

And then in the middle of June, before we went on holiday, Sigge started banging his head against the buggy. He does this when he gets angry or sad, which is pretty often. He was simply exhausted after a whole year at daycare with only a short Christmas break and now he needed a holiday. But we did not understand that then, instead we worried about his behaviour, something we had never experienced before.

Normally Sigge is neither particularly angry nor cranky. Now he did not want to play, or tease or cuddle. He ran around like a thundercloud and banged his head against a wall every now and then when we told him to come and get dressed.

We went to Gotland two weeks later, where we had rented a house for three weeks, and the first morning Sigge stopped banging his head. He woke up like a ray of sunshine and wanted to hug us and explore the anthill which was in the tree in the corner of the garden.

It was really so silly. After a difficult year in our marriage we just kept on working, becoming ever more irritated and exhausted, instead of pausing and realizing that the three of us needed time together.

How stupid can you be? What kind of stupid choices are we making anyway? Choosing strange priorities with devastating consequences that can destroy everything that has meaning.

In the evenings, after Sigge had fallen asleep, we sat close together in a hammock and talked and looked out over the fields. It took a long, long time before it was too cold to sit outside. We looked at each in wonder and asked why we hadn't done this earlier. We were surprised and happy that we had so much we wanted to talk about, almost like we were getting to know each other all other again.

During the day we biked to the ocean and we made love every afternoon when Sigge took his nap. In the house there on Gotland we had time to heal some of the wounds that had been opened, or rather we made time for each other – something we seem to be devastatingly bad at under normal circumstances.

Now, lying here in the deck chair, I just got a text message from my boss Richard at the radio station. I sent him a text earlier today asking something about work. I was struck by a pang of anxiety in the face of all of the work which will be waiting for me when I get back home next week. And now Richard had replied.

'Darling! You shouldn't be thinking about work right now. I'll take care of it! Good that you're enjoying yourself, you definitely deserve it. Hugs from a cold and grey Stkhlm!'

The awkward thing is that thoughtfulness like this makes me weep. I do not quite know why, but I start to blubber and I feel small. I have not really been mothered, as therapist Niklas would probably suggest. Yes, that is probably what it is, but I have been fathered even less. But that is not really something you can talk about, because there is not a psychological term describing a father's care for his children, maybe because no great achievements are ever expected of them?

In any case, Richard and orange men. There is some hope for the male of the species after all.

This morning at breakfast I saw the gesticulating man again, the one I had thought looked so nice. But this morning I looked at him up close. He was on his way to get some coffee when he passed my table, and I discovered that he was walking with a zombie stare and a back that was far too straight. He was patrolling the tables like an old military man, whistling with a stern look on his face. His wife was hobbling after him (strange that I did not see her limping the other day) and when she passed my table I discovered that she has a hearing aid! That is the reason for his wild gesticulating. He doesn't have a choice!

Sometimes the jigsaw pieces fall into place and I cannot help but laugh. Maybe it is due to the fact that the red wine was unusually good tonight and that I am sitting here on my balcony, newly bathed and stuffed with food, watching the sun sink behind the volcano of Mount Teide. Or maybe it is just because the bitter bitch in me has a right to her cynical observations?

I remember reading a newspaper article with the headline 'Listening to women *is* difficult'. The introduction read, 'Now you have an excuse for why you never listen to your wife. According to British researchers, it's harder to listen to women than men.' I thought about the excluding term of address, 'Now *you* have an excuse as to why *you* never listen to *your* wife.' They did not even bother to pretend that they were addressing both female and male readers.

Then a fantastic circular argument was presented, in which psychologists at Sheffield University had studied men's ability to listen to women without losing their concentration. And lo and behold: it showed that men had a harder time listening to women than to men! The reporter had even interviewed one of the researchers, who stated that women make use of language's melody in a way that makes their voices harder to listen to. Of course, the article was written by a man, and I cannot help wondering what this article would have been like if it had been written by a woman: 'It has been proven, men *are* stupid. Now you have an explanation as to why your husband never listens to you. Men have a harder time concentrating which, according to British researchers, is due to a small genetic brain imperfection.'

As luck would have it there are female researchers and they often arrive, as if by chance, at other conclusions. In *It's Called Love*, my favourite *über alles* Carin Holmberg writes about the phenomenon of not being listened to. She has interviewed tons of (heterosexual) couples about all aspects of their relationships. Among many other things, she asked how they listen to each other. And just think, the men explained that they find it harder to listen than their girlfriends/partners. The girlfriends, on the other hand, say they understand why their husbands find it difficult to listen, because they tend to bring up things which are unimportant or uninteresting!

'Personally she thinks that she's a good listener. This of course should be seen as meaning that he doesn't talk very often.'

The entire book is a searing confrontation and a detailed study of the everyday inequality and power imbalance between men and women. One of Holmberg's theories is that the voluntary subordination by women makes men's superiority invisible, to both of them. We constantly parry, cover up and take on roles and household chores 'voluntarily' like that of the dependent wife or an alcoholic. It is a line of reasoning to which I have no trouble relating. Acknowledging that men are oppressed is painful and something I would gladly postpone. . .

But what really hurts is when Carin Holmberg asks why *men aren't more bothered by their voluntary superiority?*

If I were white and living in South Africa under apartheid and started a relationship with a black man it would torture me endlessly that we, according to that culture, were not considered equals. If, despite the obstacles, I continued loving him, I would dedicate my life to fighting against apartheid.

Love – the greatest and most beautiful of all powers, the one that can truly heal wounds and change people for the better.

Why is it that men, in the name of love, fail to do everything within their power to fight against the injustices, against patriarchal apartheid? And if they see the power and thousands of years of patriarchal oppression as something which is too difficult for them to change, how is it that they do not struggle against the injustices within their own relationships? As they say, power corrupts. But does this apply to men as a group, too?

Society and culture sanctions marriage in all possible, crazy ways, something which is still, in some way, an explanation for the fact that women find themselves on the losing end of things. When it comes to caring for, loving and making time for a new little person, anybody who has children knows that two parents are less than ideal. On the other hand, three or

four would be just about right. Then there would always someone around while the rest are catching up on sleep, making
love, cooking, cleaning, shopping, working. If you ignore the
oppression gay people experience, I think the rainbow families,
the dykes and the fags, who get together and become parents,
in many ways feel much better than straight people who just
keep on struggling.

This afternoon I walked down to the ocean. I stood there,
taking deep breaths, and I felt happy, until two young men
on Vespas drove by, stopped twenty metres away from where
I was standing, turned around, drove back and parked two
metres away from me. I remained standing there, pretending
not to notice. I told myself to keep enjoying, something that
lasted about thirty seconds. By this time they had moved so
close to me that I could not ignore them any longer so I gave
up and left. They yelled something in Spanish after me but I
just kept on walking.

In the evening I tried walking to the neighbouring village of
Santa Ursula for dinner. At times like these I see the limitations of travelling alone. At the little pizzeria, which was a
bit dodgy looking, three men and I sat spread out at different
tables.

When I raised my beer glass to take a drink I suddenly saw
out of the corner of my eye one of the younger men lift his
glass as if to say cheers. I did not want to seem rude so I carefully returned the gesture and smiled what I hoped was a cool
smile. I really should not have done that. He immediately
started speaking wildly in Spanish with the other men and
then laughed a he-he laugh. I understood all too well what it
meant. Dammit.

I suddenly remembered the shock I had experienced as a sixteen year old when I was travelling around Spain by train with three girlfriends and we suddenly saw that two teenagers were standing a few metres from our table, masturbating. They were staring at us the whole time, unashamed. I strongly doubt that a man sitting alone has ever experienced something similar, either a woman masturbating openly or he-he laughs directed at his table. I strongly doubt that men can comprehend the discomfort or fear involved in having to deal with it.

I wonder how this really affects women, deep down. I assume that if anyone were ever interested in researching this they would end up with a shocking result.

For safety's sake I took a taxi back to the hotel. Once back in my room I felt how cold I was. I ran a hot bath and listened to my beloved Nina Simone and became warm down to my bones. I fell asleep like this, comfortable, warm and safe.

800 DEGREES

It is raining on Tenerife today and the mood at breakfast is just as dreary as the weather outside. The situation is made even worse by the fact that I forgot to put my contacts in, and everything is just a fuzzy mist. I'm only able to watch a German family at the table closest to me.

The woman looks terribly sad. Not just a general distant sadness like so many of the women here, but with eyes that are really red from crying sad. It looks like she's only just stopped crying. The man, who is twice her size, is chewing methodically on his ham sandwich. They have a young son who is about eight years old, and he is trying to cheer them up by telling some German jokes I do not understand. Both parents smile crookedly at him so he will not get even more worried, but you can see that he is really sad too.

Their sadness is infectious and I realize that I am suddenly feeling anxious as well. So I try and concentrate on the book I have brought with me to breakfast, *The Collected Works of Subcomandante Marcos*. It helps to read it when the every day feels petty and I need a little distance from my life. Subcomandante Marcos is the spokesman for the Zapatista guerillas in Chiapas, Mexico. In the Zapatistas Army, men and women fight alongside one another for peace, democracy and equality for the unbelievably poor indigenous people. Marcos writes about their struggle in his texts, which are both poetic and political.

On March 8, 1996 Marcos writes:

> It appears that dignity is contagious, and it is the women who are most likely to become infected with this uncomfortable ill . . . This is a good time to remember and to give their rightful places to the insurgent Zapatistas, the women who are armed and unarmed. To remember the rebels and those uncomfortable Mexican women now bent over knitting that history which, without them, is nothing more than a badly made fable. Tomorrow . . . If there is to be one, will be made with the women, and, above all, by them.'

It is easy to romanticize the Zapatistas when they have a subcomandante who writes so beautifully. I'm sure you would find many faults in the feminism of Marcos and the other male Zapatistas if you lived with them for a few weeks, but still, how can you not be grateful? They are at least demonstrating the possibility of men and women fighting together against injustice.

It is both predictable and yet still terribly annoying that in affluent Sweden, men are notable for their silence and their absence from the struggle for equality between the sexes. Hiding behind the myth of the equal Sweden is easy, but it is really just a way of denying that injustice exists, something they gladly do with the aid of personal experience, a twisted travesty of the women's movement's credo that 'The private is political.' By doing so men can, for example, claim that the statistics on battered women are exaggerated, something one of Sweden's most well-known male journalists said in an interview once: he personally only knew of one case of domestic violence among his friends and family.

A few years ago I got a job on a new community TV programme for young viewers aged between twenty and thirty-five, which the leading channel SVT would be producing. Filled with expectation, I drove out to the hotel in the archipelago for a two day conference at which the editorial staff would get to meet each other for the first time. We were also supposed to bounce around thoughts and ideas for the upcoming programme.

When a group of men and women who do not know each other meet, the women fall silent while the men develop verbal diarrhoea. That is what it was like in my film studies class at university when we had large lectures of 120 people. Most of the girls sat quietly taking notes and occasionally asking a question, while several of the boys would embark on a pseudo-dialogue with the lecturer. They rarely asked questions; instead they made statements. They often repeated what the lecturer had just said in their own words, presenting it as though it was their own observation. And strangely enough, the lecturer often went along with it, especially if she was a woman, nodding in agreement and saying, 'Hm . . . that's interesting.'

A similar situation occurred in the conference room in the hotel in the archipelago. The girls sat quietly, despite the fact that we were all smart women with several years of experience within journalism, while the men tossed their opinions around. They joked loudly while we laughed politely and encouragingly at all of their thoughts and ideas.

In the end my behaviour made me want to puke, but I am too well brought up for that so instead I boiled with rage. I felt it swell inside me, my eyes narrowed and I wished I were brave enough to test my random ideas in front of everyone, loud and proud. Finally I could not hold it in any longer. I let go and my anger boiled over. I had several ideas I wanted to try out, but in this situation I was forced to run with the most radically feminist one.

'I have a piece which I would very much like to do . . .' I said *interrupting* one of my male colleagues who was in the process of explaining how important it was for *us not to be so politically correct.*

Everyone grew quiet and slowly turned to look at me. I took a deep breath as a Vaxholm's ferry blew its horn ominously outside the window. I immediately realized this was unwelcome, and that my voice was shrill and loud.

I could feel my neck turning red and blotchy. Everyone stared at me as I tried to explain my idea for a piece about how all military resources are invested in fighting international terrorism. But imagine if the entire defence budget were used to fight all abuse, all of the rapes and murders committed by men against women every day?

No one said a word, and everyone stared.

'A report which turns the concept of international terrorism on its head . . .' I tried clarifying.

Seconds of compact silence slowly crumbled the weak courage I had managed to muster.

The male producer looked at me sceptically and uttered the phrase I would later hear every time I presented a new idea, 'I don't really understand what you mean.'

Obviously he had not had any difficulty understanding any

of the ideas that had been presented by the men throughout the day. I tried to explain and expand on my idea in a vain attempt at getting someone to nod in agreement, but everyone was sitting quietly, staring, and the male producer had, with his expression of doubt, opened up even more questions. Some of the men followed suit.

'I mean these so-called unknown cases that everyone's always talking about; it's really just the opposite when it comes to rape. Most so-called rapes aren't, because the line between consensual intercourse and rape can be pretty fine,' said one man (who by the way had been awarded a big journalism prize).

'I'm actually a bit offended that you seem to think all men are rapists!' said another. The discussion was taking off, the mood was vicious and I was history. This continued late into the night and then, after a few glasses of wine, my neighbour at the table (yet another prize-winning and well-known documentary maker) came out with another familiar statement.'

'So this thing with rape is actually really difficult, I mean, who hasn't been horny at some point and kept pushing even though the girl didn't really want it?'

I had always complained about the veteran bosses at Swedish Radio – now I realized they were harmless compared to these young cocks. A year of struggle followed, one filled with a longing for understanding and an even greater disappointment when I failed to get it.

While my male colleagues surfed along on encouragement and well-meaning understanding, my female colleagues and I wrote small pieces packed with facts before we even dared to present an idea. Seeing how it affected my self-esteem was both interesting and painful. When you are constantly met with scepticism and furrowed brows, it is impossible not to start to doubt yourself, your ideas and your abilities.

Once again I became the bitter bitch with fiery eyes who longed to be just as sloppy and spontaneous in her thoughts and ideas as the men, to be able to walk up to the producers and editors (I always had to make an appointment to present a new idea) and say, 'Hey, I saw a lemon in the cafeteria today. Wouldn't it be fun to do something on lemons? I haven't really thought it through yet, but you know what I mean, don't you?'

I longed to hear, 'That sounds like a really fun idea. We'll have a look together and come up with an angle for it.'

In situations like these it is important to keep things in perspective, so I tried not to bury myself in self-hate and self-doubt. As luck would have it, the system sometimes reveals itself. This time things became clear when two of my female colleagues presented an idea which the editor and the producers dismissed as uninteresting.

One of our male colleagues heard about it, thought it sounded really good and wanted to try running it again. He went to the editors and the producers on his own and presented the same idea as his female colleagues had just had turned down. And by chance both the editor and producers now suddenly thought it was a fabulous idea for our television programme. (We were often told that our idea did not quite match the target audience.)

It also became clear when my male colleagues suddenly got full-time positions while I got to continue working part-time.

It went on like this for an entire year, a year filled with stomach aches and a feeling of general worthlessness, until my contract ended and shockingly enough was not renewed. I felt quite relieved at my farewell dinner; it had been such a prestigious job that I had not had the strength or the courage to quit. If I'd been asked to stay I doubt I'd have said no. Or as my sensible therapist would say, 'You've found yourself in an abusive relationship and now the man who was abusing you broke it off. Be grateful!'

The entire editorial staff was invited to a nice bar at Stureplan in Stockholm. I was surrounded by some of my male colleagues for the last time and SVT treated us to food and wine and we drank and ate way too much. I ended up next to a man I had not spoken to very much during the past year. On paper he had been listed as a reporter, but he had not done a single piece in all that time. In the beginning he'd talked about doing a piece on Iran, but for some reason it had not panned out, or as he said now, 'I'm not suited to doing short and sweet reports, I'm more into portraying documentary events and processes . . .'

Men have such an amazing ability to transform their flaws into assets by bragging!

His way of speaking was reminiscent of the actor Mikael Persbrandt, his relaxed way of just releasing words impetuously yet still with nonchalance. He was about the same age as Persbrandt, had worked with art galleries in New York for a long time, and lived with one of Sweden's most well-known female designers. He was, in other words, a bigwig. Now he was sitting next to me, raising his glass of red wine to say cheers.

'Sara, it's been great getting to know you.'

'OK,' I said, truly surprised.

'Yes, it's been fun having you push your ideas. I've actually learned a lot about feminism from your pieces.'

'Oh . . .' I said, even more surprised.

'But I don't agree with everything you feminists stand for.'

'No, I can imagine,' I said, no longer as surprised.

'Just as everyone, especially feminists, assumes I visit prostitutes because I have a flat in Bangkok.'

'It's a shame they see it that way,' I replied.

'Yeah, because it's probably been at least ten years since I've been with a prostitute.'

I checked to see if he was pulling my leg, but he did not move a muscle, just took yet another gulp of his red wine.

'What?' I said, and laughed a little to show that I could take a joke. 'Do you seriously mean that you've gone to see Thai prostitutes?'

'Yes, but now I can see you're a bit upset by it. You should know that I've never been with a prostitute while I've been in a relationship with someone. I've never been unfaithful to any of my girlfriends,' he said, and looked at me wide-eyed as if to emphasize what an honourable fellow he was.

'But I don't care if you were unfaithful. People can screw around as much as they want, but I do care when I hear that you took advantage of poor Thai women who are forced into prostitution as the only means of survival. What does it feel like to fuck someone who has to do it for the money but isn't the least bit interested?' I asked angrily.

'Now it's not that simple, saying that they aren't up for it,' he said, and I looked him in the eye again to see if he was kidding.

Apparently he saw how serious I was because now he started almost pleading with me.

'Have you ever been to Thailand?'

'No,' I said. He nodded in confirmation.

'No, I didn't think so! It's pretty hard to understand if you haven't been there. It's a different culture when it comes to these things.'

'You don't mean that prostitution is ingrained in Thai society?' I said, and felt how my voice rose shrilly, all the way to the top of my throat.

'This is bloody hard to explain to someone who has never been there, but these are girls who don't want to stand and sweat in a factory sixteen hours a day, so they have chosen an easier way to make money.'

'Just stop. I don't want to hear any more,' I said and drank three quick gulps of my red wine.

Just then the male producer came over to our end of the table and sat down.

'Listen, do you two realize that everyone thinks you're hitting on each other? You've been sitting here talking for a damn long time and everyone thinks you're getting together.'

He was talking nonsense and was struggling to focus.

'Nope, we've just been talking and Sara is pretty angry with me,' my colleague said, staring down at the table.

'Whaa?' the male producer said and grinned so wide his snuff patch could be glimpsed where it was hanging, staining his teeth black. You get what you ask for, I thought to myself.

'Dennis was just telling me he used to visit Thai prostitutes and I became pretty upset about it,' I said and stared at the male producer. His eyes went wide and for a second he managed to focus before quickly getting up and walking to the toilets without saying a word.

My male colleague got up too and went and sat at the other end of the table. I remained sitting alone and felt the tears burning in my eyes. Fuck. Do not start crying now, not now, do not start crying now, lampshade, lampshade, lampshade.

But it was late and I was too drunk, so I biked home in the cold spring night and cried so hard I was forced to stop below the castle and walk my bike. I looked up at the men in uniform who were standing, guarding the castle in stiff positions, and I thought about the poor king and his poor queen and their poor children. What a fake life, those poor, poor, fools!

I sat down and rested on the edge of the footpath and thought about all the games we're always playing and how hard it is to be straight and honest and, most of all, how hard it is to be honest with yourself. I cried about all of the damned Johns, all the male producers, veteran bosses and all the female producers and editors who play the same male game. (There is a special place in hell for women who don't help each other!) I cried about all my boyish journalist colleagues. I cried because I was drunk and I cried about being human.

The circle was complete and when I finally got up from the footpath and started biking home I had stopped crying and started to realize what a shitty place I had been in for the last year. Or, if one is going to be honest: what a shitty place I find myself in every day that I work as a journalist.

There are statistics on several other professions – evidence that women only get part-time positions while their male colleagues get full-time ones, permanent positions, better pay, etc etc . . .

Women medical students are forced to be four times more qualified than their male counterparts in order to get research positions. Of course the same holds true for journalism, but oddly enough there has not been a study of journalism or the media yet.

I am really trying to find my worth. To *feel* my worth. I just wish it did not require so much effort. It is as if it does not matter how many prizes I get, how many good reviews, what I feel is furious: peacock.

'Hampus! Cornelia!' a woman is yelling in desperation at her two small children who are wildly chasing each danger-ously close to the edge of the pool. She is trying to make eye contact with her husband but he is busy inspecting his beer bottle, a Heineken, which they sell cheaply here in the hotel's *Supermercado*.

You see lots of fathers drinking beer by the pool here at La Quinta Park while the mothers run around madly after their children. There are always struggling women and distant men, and pure and simple anxiety. What would happen if women just said enough is enough! When I see the man start on his fourth Heineken, I cannot resist a bit of wishful thinking: leave now, lady!

I think about Mum. Beloved Mum! A rough diamond who never realized what exists inside of her. Maybe with different parents, different big brothers, she would have understood. If she had realized her value as a diamond maybe she would have left Dad the first time he said how worthless and ugly she was, looked at him as if he were crazy and calmly said, 'No one talks to me like that. Pack your bags and get out.'

Instead she kept on doing the dishes with her back turned towards Dad, towards us. And Dad continued yelling and now I am sitting here at the edge of the pool watching Heineken Dad, realizing just how angry I am at him. Not so much because he was an absent, second-rate father, I could have lived with that. But because of all the horrible things he said to Mum.

There is a raw justice in the fact that, being the one who took care of us all those years, she has the best relationship with us now. She always took care of the social contacts with friends and family and she also got to keep in touch with them. She is even in touch with my Grandma, his mother, and his sisters Kristina and Solveig. I think Dad on the other hand has never sent a birthday card during his entire adult life.

Mum is a living example of what we know, that women often blossom when they get divorced, while men suddenly realize how lonely they are. Men pay a price for their superiority as well. That must be a difficult pill to swallow when you have had everything served to you on a platter for so many years. Now he sits there, my father, alone and helpless in his attempts at staying in touch with his children, who respond only out of politeness. Is he filled with guilt? Does he realize anything? Or is he just a happy mess of forgetfulness and suppressed feelings?

Maybe he cries at night. Just like that time, when I was little, and I saw him crying over the popcorn. Back then, a long, long time ago, he could comfort me when I was sad. I will not forget that. But I also will not forget how he frightened me when he tormented Mum. How afraid I was of him. How he always remained a father I could not count upon. A father with a dark side which sometimes made him cross the line.

The anxiety I feel as an adult is the same as that of my childhood. It is an abyss which opens up and I have no idea how I am going to get across. Pitch black darkness in a vacuum.

And deep down inside there is a bottomless longing for the safe father who would comfort me. But my disappointment is bottomless too, and it stands in the way of reconciliation. That is why I sound like an operator when I talk to him every now and then. And because he has never sent a birthday card to me I have also stopped sending them to him. I just call and say Happy Birthday.

Birthdays make all the crap visible. A colleague at the radio station, a woman in her fifties, said to me one day, 'When it's his birthday I'm the one who cleans the flat, invites everyone, does the shopping, makes the food and buys the presents. When it's my birthday, I'm the one who cleans the flat, invites everyone, does the shopping, makes the food and buys the presents.'

When it was Mum's birthday, Dad reluctantly dragged himself out of bed only after Kajsa and I had woken him with silent, persistent poking. He finally came down to the kitchen where we had already made breakfast and set it on a tray. We had picked purple violets which Mum had planted in the front garden in order to hide everything that was missing. Then we went upstairs and sang as loudly as we could in order to drown out Dad's silence.

Mum still says that she doesn't want anything for her birthday. But even the little things make her happy. All of the horrible years she lived through have made it so that she still stands at the counter with her back to us, vacuuming, peeling potatoes, or has bread rising at the same time as she is taking a gulp of her lukewarm coffee and a drag on her cigarette. She has a hard time just being and thinks her only worth lies in serving and cleaning.

Lasse, her partner for the last ten years, is nice and wants the best for her. He watches TV, walks the dog, is unhappy with his job, plays golf and reads the evening paper. He sits in his very own TV chair and asks, 'What are we having for dinner?'

And Mum answers proudly, 'Pork loin and potato wedges.'

I think they have a good life together – despite the ancient pattern which seems impossible to change.

It still hurts to see her though, and I wish she could understand how wonderful she is. I wish she understood how grateful I am to her for always being there. I am grateful because she came up with things to do, skiing outings in the winter and swimming in the summer, and because she sometimes made hot chocolate with whipped cream for us for breakfast. She sewed a Madicken apron for me when my primary school celebrated its one hundredth anniversary. She came to the parent-teacher conferences, and the chats, and sometimes she made real banana-shaped pastries. I am grateful because she was happy so often, even though things must have been so difficult.

Sometimes she is just as eccentric as Isadora's red-headed mother, laughs loudly and disco dances. Then I am so infinitely proud of her, of my inheritance. I have not been robbed of everything.

When I see her chasing Sigge on the jungle gym, I am grateful too. She laughs, overjoyed that she's a pirate! She takes great pains to climb up to him, while all of the other Grandmas remain standing on the ground, watching on, embarrassed. Maybe they think she is a bit over the top? She yells and shouts after Sigge. I hear her loud, shrill voice across the entire park and it makes me warm all over. Or like when she sang karaoke at my aunt's fiftieth birthday party, even though she is tone deaf.

My aunt Ulla had rented a karaoke machine for the party and was looking forward to her guests letting lose, but no one, not a single one of the guests, a religious, frightened gathering of selfish souls, wanted to sing, despite the fact that they sing in the church choir every damn Sunday. I love my aunt and I was filled with such contempt towards all of those mean, quiet people.

Finally Mum went up and belted out 'Four Jigs and a Coca-cola', tone deaf as she is, and it was fantastic. None of the guests applauded, they just looked at each like they were about to puke. It was shocking. I was so angry I asked one of the old bags who looked the worst off if she was feeling unwell.

'No,' she said uncertainly, with a sour expression. Of course I realized it was not very kind of me to ask, but I was forced to defend Mum against all those evil looks.

(Later in the evening I got mine when I heard that old bag had been left by her husband and was in remission after battling cancer . . . shame on you Sara!)

My cousins, and aunt Ulla and aunt Kristine and I were the only ones who yelled 'Bravo!' when Mum sang. And then we took turns, defying all of the ill will, and belted out our joy.

I passionately sang Ebba Grön's '800 Degrees, You can count on me, you can count on me'. I jumped up and down like a punk rocker in Ulla's tiny living room. Mum was doubled over on the floor laughing her shrill, loud laugh. She was laughing at me. It was a big moment in my life. Then we realized that almost the entire party had moved out on to Ulla's balcony in order to avoid hearing us, but we had gone crazy and just continued singing and howling.

'All Shook Up', 'Let's Go to the Hop', 'I Will Survive', 'Good Vibrations'.

At eleven o'clock the last of the religious ones had gone home, there was tons of sparkling wine left and we continued late into the night, singing for each other, drunk on our own greatness.

There in the living room, when I saw my mother dancing crazily, singing to Elvis, I was filled with an endless pride.

My brave, cocky, happy mother who does not give a damn about all of those damn, cruel people.

No, I definitely have not been stripped of everything.

I SAY GOODBYE
(1993)

It is my last year at home, and in August after school has finished I am moving to Stockholm. Mum and Dad are not talking to each other, except when Dad is drunk and then he just yells. My room is at the other end of the house so I do not hear the words, just the commotion.

Most nights I stay at Jens's or Micke's or with one of my other boyfriends who has their own flat. It is calm and quiet there and I can come and go as I please. In their beds I get to lie close, close by, enclosed in their embraces.

Sometimes I bike home to eat and get clean clothes. Mum is desperate; every time I return she asks me to sleep at home.

'I don't want you to be gone so much!' she says, holding on to my leather jacket.

Harshly, I bend back her dry eczema hands that refuse to let go, rush to my bike and yell 'Bye!' as I bike off into the night.

I cannot put up with all of the yelling and all of the silence; with Dad who is disappearing all of the time, going away, coming home at strange hours, or in the middle of the night. Or with Mum trying to maintain some form of normality, but she cries just a little too often, in the middle of the day, or in the evening when I am about to leave.

I bike away, away, and every night I am happy and beautiful and drunk at Doctor Z's. All of my boyfriends and the other night owls who gladly stay up until the place closes at three o'clock are there.

One night I come home and find Mum and Dad's bed empty. It has been several days since I stayed at home and I walk around our empty house, searching. I look in on my sleeping little brother and little sister. But there is no Dad and no Mum. It starts to give me the creeps and I realize I am shaking as I open various doors, afraid of what I will find. There are no boundaries any more; I know that anything is possible.

I finally find Mum sleeping on a camp bed in the little sewing room she has set up for herself. I am relieved to see her there, sleeping, unharmed.

'Mum!' I say and shake her. 'Wake up! I'm home now!'

She sits up with a jerk and looks at me with frightened eyes.

'OK, good,' she says after a few seconds.

'Where's Dad?' I ask.

'I don't know!' she answers, irritated.

'Good night then!' I say and I go to my room and change into my pyjamas.

When I lock the door to my room it suddenly hits me. I did not ask her why she was sleeping on the camp bed and not in their bed. I pull the covers over my face. I did not ask, because I do not want to know.

I dream that I am swimming in a deep pool. Suddenly I see my little brother lying on the bottom. I try to swim down to him but it is too deep and I can only make it about ten feet. I reach out with my arms for all I am worth but I cannot reach him and I keep having to surface for air.

The pool is filled with other swimmers and I cry and scream for them to help me. Some of them try, but the pool is too deep for them too, and I see my little brother becoming more and more lifeless down there.

I try again and this time I see that the bottom is covered with drowned children. The whole pool is a mass grave and I give up and swim towards the edge, crying. I try not to look down, but I am still filled with disgust at having to swim over the children's bodies.

More and more often I wake up in the morning to discover that my pillow is soaked with sweat and tears.

I hate secondary school and the only reason I go is my friends, Ylva, Cissi, Annie and Sanna. We do all of the group projects together at Hallström's Café where you get free refills and we drink coffee until we get the shakes. Poisoned with caffeine, we hold long, lengthy discussions about Cuba and Castro and the class system.

The teachers smell my clothes which always stink from the smoke and the bar, maybe they sense my underprivileged background? Maybe they suspect my dysfunctional family? They have started to use a condescending, tired tone when they speak to me and not the expectant one they had in the beginning when I arrived from middle school with such good grades.

One evening as I am wobbling home from Doctor Z's I meet a boy from school. He is doing sciences and we do not know each other, but I know that his name is Oskar and that he lives in a charming suburb right outside the city. Just as I pass him on the footpath he hisses 'Damned communist whore!' But I am drunk and I just wobble on, laughing.

The next day I see the students who are doing the two year vocational course, sitting smoking in one corner of the school playground. They have the lowest status at the school and everyone despises them for their laziness and misfortune. I see Oskar walk by with his friends, with their slick-backed hair and expensive jackets. They say something to the smokers and laugh crudely, and I suddenly realize that Oskar and his friends are looking at me. These days I belong with the misfits. In their eyes I am a loser and I start to suspect they are right.

All of us gather in the school choir room. Oskar and his middle-class friends, the skippers from the social track who do not want to miss the opportunity to miss class and then people like me and my friends. We are standing somewhere to the left of centre: the culturally interested communist whores. We are a motley crew singing as loudly as we can in order to reduce the disorder. It is almost the festival of St Lucia and we are singing about stars shining over the baby Jesus. It is a tradition. Another tradition at our secondary school with its one-hundred-year-old roots is that the star boys clown about just enough so that it is hilarious but not so much that it gets out of control. The boys from sciences are always the star boys, the boys from the social track are the elves and they do not participate in the fun. Instead they get to stand off to the side, smiling stupidly, just like us, St Lucia's attendants.

The science boys usually change the words to 'Staffan Was a Stable Boy' so that the meaning is different and some of them wear funny hats instead of the usual white star-boy hats. It is funny and entertaining and the entire auditorium, filled with teachers and students, laughs at them. Every year it is the same, and during my last year of secondary school it is Oskar and his friends who are getting ready. We hear them discussing the text, hear them laughing at their own jokes.

We stand there next to them, stupid and obedient, practising silly songs about stupid Jesus, and getting more and more annoyed. Until one day it becomes unbearable. We are sitting, getting the coffee shakes at Hallström's and Ylva is complaining about how pathetic she feels. She is beautiful with long, dark hair and it is obvious that she is going to be the school's Lucia since she sings beautifully too. But today everything is horribly depressing.

Maybe it is because Oskar and his star boys were singing their version of 'Staffan Was a Stable Boy' during rehearsal, which they had renamed 'Steffo's Stupid Gang', in their proud voices and the entire choir was laughing. Then it was our turn to sing 'A Star is Shining' and suddenly everything became so obvious and boring.

All of us suffer as we drink even more coffee. We are particularly sympathetic towards Ylva, who is the one standing at the very front, representing this shit. And how did it happen anyway, Annie asks, that the cool gorgeous girls got turned into Christian girls?

'We who were once proud communist whores . . .' I say, and Cissi goes and gets the coffee pot and fills our cups again.

Sanna has been sitting quietly but now she starts waving her hands with excitement.

'I know!' she says. 'Let's get all of the attendants and we'll stage a Lucia coup!'

And that is why in an empty classroom one dark Lucia morning, Lucia and her attendants are making themselves look pregnant, stuffing pillows under their shapeless white night-gowns and tying their glittery sashes so that their stomachs are round and very obvious. We help each other put on make-up, bright red lipstick and smeared, green eye shadow. Whore make-up.

At seven-thirty we slowly walk into the packed auditorium and sing as beautifully as we can. I look for a reaction amongst the faces in the auditorium, but everyone stares blankly. No one is smiling and no one is laughing. Then it is time for the star boys' solo. Oskar and his friends take three steps forward and start singing their 'Steffo's Stupid Gang'. The lyrics are about them wanting to drink beer rather than eat porridge, sleep in rather than go to the Lucia procession and more than anything else, have their own attendant to hug. *We thank them so much.* The audience, teachers and students, break into hysterical laughter. Aren't they easily amused. Then it is our turn. Ylva takes a step forward and twenty very pregnant attendants start singing 'aaaoooomm . . . aaooommm'.

We have borrowed the melody from 'The Moose are Demonstrating' and sing:

> The attendants are demonstrating
> The attendants have had enough
> The attendants want to have some fun
> Here in their own procession
> Aaaooommm . . .
> Aaoooommmm

Ylva takes out a megaphone and yells out into the auditorium: 'My attendants demand a more exciting Lucia procession!'

And the whole time we hum a steady:

> Aaooommm
> Aaaooommm
> Aaooommm
> Aaaooommm

Then it becomes quiet. Ylva takes a step back and we wait, for something. And it is still quiet, until the music teacher hits the beginning note for the Lucia song with difficulty and again we're forced to sing that damned beautiful song in our soprano voices. All while slowly walking out between the rows of eyes which are still staring at us, blankly.

> Dreams filled with the sound of wings
> Prophecy above us
> Santa Lucia
> Santa Lucia

We stand in the empty classroom we use as a dressing room and Ylva tears off her crown of candles, the wax dripping on her long hair. A large map of the world is hanging on the wall and someone put a used snuff patch on the map to mark New York.

'Damned silly boring idiots!' she hisses. Sanna rubs her shoulders and Cissi orders us to hurry up for Christ's sake!

Then we walk quietly as a group through the sleet in our shitty little town, to Anne's house. There, in the basement, we get out our rum and coke. It is nine-thirty in the morning, and we pass the bottle around as we each take three quick gulps. Around and around until we can no longer stand and then we lie down, entangled in a pile on the floor. We play The Clash, 'Know Your Rights' on the stereo so loudly that it pounds and occupies our heads. Everything is pounding and I have time to think *this is beautiful* before I doze off, completely safe.

The spring is cold and I would die were it not for my friends. I would die if I could not get the closeness which awaits me in the beds of my boyfriends. It is warm and calm there, and I make love to all of them, one after another.

I am biking home from school one day when my tyre suddenly blows. I jump off and start to walk and I am about to turn on my Walkman when I see Dad come by on a shiny new silver bike. We catch sight of each other and stare in surprise; I have not been home for a week.

'I've got a flat tyre,' I tell him curtly, because I do not know what else to say. Talking to him in calm, everyday circumstances like this feels strange.

'I see,' he says while chewing his gum, which he thinks will hide the alcohol on his breath.

'Have you bought a new bike?' I ask.

'Yes, I have. Eighteen speeds. It wasn't cheap but I thought a new bike would be a good idea,' he says, and I think about Mum's old rusty one speed, which she has had for more than fifteen years now. The one she took us to daycare on during all the years that Dad had the car. On cold, early winter mornings she would wrap us in blankets and push the bike through the slush, Kajsa on the parcel rack and me on the handlebars; it was cosy sitting there like that, wrapped in a blanket, heavy with morning tiredness. A red, second-hand bike which she loads down with shopping bags and still creaks around on.

'Did you buy it today?' I ask.

'Yes and I've been to the tanning salon for the first time in my life,' he says and laughs, a bit embarrassed.

Something in me breaks and after a moment I realize that it is contempt. I despise him so much and I cannot help it, it flows through my entire body. In front of me I see him lying on the tanning bed sweating like a pig with a small grin on his face, while Mum is biking on her old, ugly red bike, rushing to pick up my brother from after-school club and do the shopping. She is probably at home now preparing dinner.

The contempt quickly flows through my veins. For all his angry outbursts that scare me, because he grabs my little brother too hard when he is yelling at him. Because he makes my little brother cry, told my little sister she was ugly when she got braces. Because he voted for the rightwing New Democracy party and for all of the racist things he has ever said about Muslims and Africans and because he is tormenting the life out of all of us with his infernal existence.

Maybe he senses my disdain, because he suddenly jumps up on his bike and says, 'Goodbye, see you at home.'

I watch him disappear and wonder what it means, why didn't he walk home with me? Something aches inside; maybe it is hatred's hangover?

At home all of us except Dad eat spaghetti with meat sauce. He is in the garage messing around with something. No one ever knows where he is or what he is doing, just that he comes and goes as he pleases at strange hours of the day. When we have finished eating I go out to the garage. I really want to stop hating him and I am ashamed of the deep hatred I felt earlier in the day. Dad is sorting out his tools, hanging them up in the right place and throwing away old junk, stuff that is broken.

'Hi Dad!' I say.

'Hi!' he says and looks at me in surprise.

'Do you want some help?' I ask, pointing at the pile of junk that needs to be thrown out.

'No,' he says and stops sorting. 'Sara . . . There's something I need to tell you . . .'

'OK, what is it?' I ask and prepare myself for the worst. It has been a long, long time since I have seen him this calm and serious. Maybe he is going to reveal that he has got cancer, which would explain his mysterious outbursts, his absence, his depression.

'Well, unfortunately your mother and I have decided to get a divorce . . .'

He looks at me expectantly, as if he is preparing himself for a strong reaction, an objection. I think about all the times I have yelled at them and said I wished they would get a divorce. Maybe he has never taken it seriously? Maybe he really thought it was best to keep things together 'for the sake of the children'?

'Good,' I say, 'you should have done it a long time ago.'

Dad looks at me in silence and bites his lip. His expression becomes hard and distant.

I try and explain. 'You haven't been happy as long as I can remember. I just do not understand why you didn't get divorced earlier.'

'OK. But now you know,' he says, as he turns his back to me and starts sorting his tools again.

I call Krille and ask him to come and get me in his car. We go to his place and he strokes my hair while I cry. He holds me until I fall asleep.

At school I get in an argument with my Swedish teacher. He is bald and has fancy corduroy trousers and he cannot hide how wonderfully different he thinks he is.

I have just discovered that our literature book does not mention any women writers other than Selma Lagerlöf. We are reading about the Modernists and I want to know why Virginia Woolf is not mentioned anywhere in the whole book, which is quite thick.

'The authors of this book,' he says in an irritated voice and with an angry expression, 'have selected writers who have had the most impact on literature.'

I know how impossible I am being, how detrimental this will be to my marks and my relationship with my classmates who already think I am difficult, but I cannot stop.

'I would like to know more about Virginia Woolf,' I say. 'She's been important for me.'

It is true. I had just read *Orlando* and was fascinated by the language and Orlando's travels through time and gender. The class sighs and my teacher sighs and says that he can make some copies of a few pages about Virginia if it is really that important to me.

'But when it comes to Modernism, Proust and Joyce are much more important!' he says, and I hate him and I start hating more and more people.

By the time my final year comes to an end I have horrible marks but I am still happy, through and through. I am filled with a feeling of freedom which I have been waiting and hungering for my entire life. I am drunk on sparkling wine from early morning until late in the night. All my relatives, old friends, neighbours and all of my old and new boyfriends come.

Everyone gets along and seems happy, even Mum and Dad. I eat sponge cake and beam, safe in the knowledge that the next morning I am leaving for a month-long backpacking trip.

The knowledge that a kind of hell is really over for me now is present in my whole body. The knowledge that something new is waiting for me, Europe and an entire life to live!

The next morning, my four best friends and I are sitting crammed into a train compartment. Our parents and siblings are crammed on to the platform. I see the dark circles under my dad's eyes and Mum's wrinkles from all that smoking. They look tired. I see my beloved little sister and wonderful little brother. I have a stab of guilt; I am saving my life and leaving them behind with Mum and Dad in hell. But I do not want the guilt to sabotage my happy feeling of freedom.

Not now.

I am also tired and long to be happy.

The train starts moving and we lean out of the window and wave.

'Bye!' I yell loudly.

'Bye!' I scream.

Goodbye you arseholes. Goodbye everyone. To hell with you.

TUFTS OF A LEOPARD

I call home to hear Sigge's voice. When I called yesterday he did not want to talk to me. But he comes to the phone today.

'Hey sweetie! It's Mummy. How are you?'

I hear his bright little voice which I love more than anything in this world.

'Hi. I'm OK. Bye!'

He runs off, disappearing; I hear his small steps on the wooden floor. It breaks my heart and I try and keep my voice steady but it goes up into a falsetto. Yet again a kind of justice: if I leave I can count on him being angry at me.

Grandma Eva is babysitting and says that she and Sigge have drawn a picture of me, Johan and Sigge riding on a boat in Tenerife, all three of us. We hang up and now I am hit with an immense longing mixed with anxiety and guilt. What have I done? What am I doing here?

I try to invoke the heavy, enormous tiredness I was walking around with in the weeks before I arrived, how disgusting I felt and much I longed for sleep and solitude. Why the hell can things never be good? I have been gone for five days. Five pitiful days! A two year old and his thirty-year-old miserable mummy should be able to survive that without too much trauma!

Nina Simone is singing 'I wish I knew how it would feel to be free'.

Yep. I wish.

There is a gym at the hotel. So often in the past when I've been sad I have thought, I am going to go and exercise. It works almost as well as a warm bath, a way of at least getting a little bit more contact with my body.

I change and go down to the gym, and it turns out that an aerobics class is about to start. Young Spanish girls with glittery shirts and leg warmers are milling around. A few have small leopard-patterned tufts of fur around their arms and wrists. Maybe the area around La Quinta Park is affluent? On my walks I have seen houses with budding gardens and locked gates for security. Yes, that is probably it. This group looks like it belongs at the Sturebadet gym in Stockholm rather than at Friskis & Svettis. At Friskis you see overweight girls wearing T-shirts bearing the slogan 'I Love Dajm!' and all sorts of untrained bodies moving together. A liberating nerdiness rules over the entire building.

The only time I have been to Sturebadet I slipped on the well-polished tiles and the older women looked at me in concern. I crawled up clumsily from the floor and felt like an outsider. Their looks made me paranoid and I wondered if I smelled, or if they thought I was a junkie who had managed to sneak in for a shower.

Here among all of these tufts of fur I get the same feeling. For a second my class hatred is ignited. I look down at my washed-out gym trousers and my discoloured, greyish and once white T-shirt. My class anxiety.

Just as I am debating whether or not to go into the gym and get on a bike, the teacher for the class comes up to me. She is about thirty-five and introduces herself as Rosita. She gives me a friendly smile and says that she hasn't seen me here before. I explain that I am a guest at the hotel and she asks for my name and says I am very welcome. Her smile is friendly and warm, so I decide to stay.

The class starts and my heart is soon pumping in time with the bad Euro-disco music. The leopard tufts and I are doing step combination after step combination. I grin happily because it feels so good, almost like dancing. Rosita grins at all of us but mostly at me.

When it is time for the strength training she comes over and shows the class which angle to use when doing sit-ups by placing her hand on the small of my back. Strangely enough the attention does not embarrass me, instead I enjoy it. It makes me feel chosen. The leopard tufts all look happy and I think that the glitter does not really matter. Let them glitter, it suits them.

I am greedily drinking from my water bottle after class when Rosita comes walking towards me.

'Sara! It was very fun to have you here! Please come tomorrow at seven, it's body toning. Lots of fun!'

I look at her in surprise. This is so unlike the Swedish shyness. I have never had a teacher come up to me like this after a training session.

'Yes. Maybe I'll come, it was great fun!' I say kindly.

'Good!' she says confidently. 'See you tomorrow!'

'OK,' I reply, surprised, and realize that I will have to show up again tomorrow.

I spend the next day in the deck chair, alternately dozing and reading. My muscles are sore which makes me limp to the pool. I clumsily throw myself in and swim a few laps. At least now I look a little bit like the retirees. Maybe the people watching me think I am here for my rheumatism? My MS? Would this give me a more valid reason for leaving my husband and child at home? Well, maybe.

When it starts getting close to seven I start getting a bit nervous. This feels awkward. What if Rosita's invitation meant something else entirely? My anxiety irritates me. Does it matter what thoughts could be behind it? After all, I like working out. Why must I get so embarrassed when people show an interest in me?

I put on my ugly exercise clothes and go down to the gym. Rosita comes up to me immediately.

'Sara! You came! Good.'

I see a new group of leopard tufts staring curiously at me.

'Yes. Hello,' I say weakly.

Rosita takes my hand and leads me into the room. Now I know I have red blotches on my neck, fiery red spots that always appear when I become so horribly embarrassed. What does she think anyway? Have I broken some sort of rule? Got involved in an agreement I did not know about by showing up here again? But the session is starting and after a while I leave all the embarrassment behind and enjoy feeling my body work.

If Rosita is embarrassed she does not show it at all. Instead she comes up again immediately after the session.

'You were fantastic Sara!' she says, and it makes me happy even if I suspect she is only saying it to flatter me.

'Thank you!' I reply.

'Do you want to have a drink with me in the bar?' she asks happily, and I assume she notes my hesitation because she continues before I get a chance to answer. 'Just a small beer. It's such fun to see a young person here at the hotel!'

She grins and I start smiling too, because there is something liberating about her open manner, even though it troubles me.

'Well, OK, just a small one!' I reply.

We decide to meet in the bar in fifteen minutes so we have time to shower. Fifteen minutes later we are sitting across from each other and each of us has a beer.

Rosita wants to know why I am here and I try and explain what January is like. What January in Sweden can do to people. She laughs and says that she does not understand because she grew up on Tenerife, and when they get a little bit of rain it usually just makes them happy.

It is actually quite fun. Rosita is inquisitive and happy. We laugh a lot and I ask what it is like to work at the gym here at La Quinta Park. Rosita says that it is OK but she gets tired of all of the retirees. She is thirty-seven and when I tell her I am thirty she is surprised that I am that old. She becomes even more surprised when I tell her that I am married and have a son.

'You don't look like a mother!' she says.

I laugh. 'And what does a mother look like then?'

'Fat!' she replies with distaste. 'That's why I don't have any children. I don't want to lose my grip.'

I look at her toned body and think that is exactly what it means to become a mother, losing your grip. No matter how toned you are, you give up your body and a part of yourself. That is why it is so painful. It is not until I manage to let go and lose control that it will become possible to enjoy motherhood. And that is why becoming a mother seems to be such an impossible project when it comes to equality.

I remember the first few months with Sigge, how every minute was spent getting him to sleep a little so that I could have a moment to myself. How I worked against him instead of enjoying his waking moments. How I had such a hard time letting go of everything, my old life, and just being in the here and now.

With embarrassment, I remember my third visit to the day-care centre. I brought a newspaper, hoping that Sigge would play by himself so that I could read in peace. The other mums were sitting on the floor as usual, half a foot from their babies. I put Sigge down and walked six feet away and sat down on a comfortable sofa. Sigge immediately started crawling around and investigating the mountain of toys and I happily opened my newspaper and started to read. I was right in the middle of an article about PM Göran Persson's leadership style when I suddenly realized that everything was quiet. All conversation had stopped and when I looked up from my paper I saw that the five floor mums were sitting there staring at me angrily. Sigge was happily gnawing on an orange plastic fish and I could not understand what was wrong. What had he done? What had I done?

I had settled down on the sofa and in doing so ended up two feet higher than the floor mums. I did what I had seen so many fathers do at the daycare centre. Apparently for a mother, doing the same thing was not OK. I tried ignoring the silence for half a minute and then I gave up, got up and sat on the floor half a foot away from Sigge.

The floor mums returned to their conversations, oh, those murderous conversations about lack of sleep, weight gain and colic! So boring, time stands still. I smiled a little at them but no one smiled back. I had clearly shown that I did not want to be one of them and now I was not welcome.

I never went back to the daycare centre again.

Now in hindsight I can almost understand them. There really was something typically dismal in my constant desire to escape. I get irritated every time I see a father with that absent look while the child screams for attention; all the dads I see reading the paper while the children are missing them. The big difference is that the absence of the father is not regarded as critically as that of the mother. And it actually makes me a little bitter bitchy. Men can become fathers without needing to forgo their selfish impulses, while women have to give up so much when they wander into the cramped room of motherhood. I see Sigge's angry eyes, his disappointment when I have been away. Even our children seem to have an inherent feeling for what demands they can place on Mum and what demands they can place on Dad.

Rosita orders two more beers for us and I thank her happily. I suddenly feel like getting really drunk and ignoring all of these hopeless thoughts.

'Can't you take me somewhere we can dance?' I ask.

'*Bueno!*' Rosita yells. 'Of course!'

We ride on her Vespa and I hold on to her waist tightly. I breathe in the sea air and close my eyes so I will not see the curves Rosita takes without slowing down.

We are at what I assume is a real Tenerife disco, meaning wonderfully horrible disco music from different decades and drinks which are much too strong. But I want to get drunk so I guzzle my gin and tonic in big gulps. Rosita laughs and pulls me out on to the dance floor.

We dance wildly, mimicking each other with big movements that create lots of space around us. Madonna is singing that she is a virgin and Bono about Bloody Sundays and we laugh at each other and compete to see who can dance the worst. I think I win.

In the end I can barely stand on my aching legs so I sit down at the bar and guzzle another gin and tonic. Rosita is dancing with one of the few men who dared to approach us. Her dancing is calmer now, more in tune with his movements.

The DJ is playing 'I'm gonna give you a lick with my razor tongue' and I see several men sticking their tongues out during the chorus and moving them quickly back and forth. Rosita looks at me and rolls her eyes, I roll mine back at her.

'I'm gonna give you a lick with my razor tongue.' I look around and try to find someone who is doing the tongue thing in a joking way, but everyone seems serious and excited. Damn reptiles.

I've had enough dancing and I walk over to Rosita and give her a big hug.

'Thank you, thank you, thank you,' I say in her ear.

Rosita just laughs and hugs me back. In the taxi on the way back I cannot stop smiling. I feel so amazingly satisfied.

I sit on the balcony for a while and look out into the night and think that life is still pretty wonderful. Right now I am a mother who is doing what she wants to, without guilt or a bad conscience.

A LITTLE TIME LEFT
(1993)

We come home from our backpacking trip one July evening, happily filthy and hungry. The last few days we have been living on bread and Italian mineral water. We have travelled non-stop from Greece in three days, slept sitting up and sweated on hot trains through Italy and Eastern Europe. But it does not matter, it is just a part of the adventure, filled as we are with our newly won adult freedom.

Mum has made potato soup and for a short while she stands next to me smiling, watching me as I hungrily down the food. There is a smile and an unusual calm about her which lures me into trying to explain and describe everything we have seen.

'The beaches of Corfu were amazing. We just lay in the sun and went swimming all day,' I say.

'Uh-huh,' she says, amused, turns around and goes to the fridge to get out a bag of cinnamon rolls.

'You would like Prague, Mum! It was so beautiful!' I say, and tell her about how we managed to get a flat in the centre of the city.

'Uh-huh,' Mum says, and puts the rolls in the microwave.

'And Rome was also beautiful, but too expensive for us. I

think I'm going to go there when I have more money. We could only afford pasta and tomato sauce, so finally we headed to Greece. It was cheap there.'

'Uh-huh,' Mum says, and puts on the coffee.

'We slept a lot on the trains so we could afford to be away longer. It went pretty well, you get used to sleeping in the chairs.' I say, and look at Mum at the sink with her back to me.

'Uh-huh,' Mum says, and sets out coffee cups and plates.

She pours herself a cup of coffee, sits down across from me and lights a cigarette. But by now I have stopped talking. Just then Dad comes in through the door. He has the evening paper under his arm and he walks over to the coffee pot and pours himself a cup.

'Well, I see you've come home,' he says, and disappears from the kitchen again with his coffee and his paper.

I look at Mum's expressionless eyes, she is staring into thin air and for a moment I wonder if she has taken too many painkillers.

'Thanks for the food!' I say, and she wakes up for a second and looks at me.

'OK,' she says, and gets up to put away the dishes.

I go to the bathroom and take a long, hot shower. I had forgotten what it was like, I think to myself. How could I forget? But four weeks with the best of friends in total freedom made me forget and be happy for a while. Uninterrupted, we talked about the future on the trains and in the hostels and the beaches and the bars. What our lives would be like and what they wouldn't be like. For four weeks we have been fantasizing non-stop about our adult lives, which lie completely within reach, waiting for us. They are grand fantasies without limitations.

I put on my dirty jeans and a black T-shirt and bike out into the night, to Doctor Z's where I know all of my boyfriends are waiting. I cannot be alone tonight, and after just one beer I see the most handsome man I have ever seen. His name is Benjamin and he is new to the area. We dance and his kisses taste like nicotine. I give him a ride to his student flat on my bike and then I make love to him with a longing which is endless.

Afterwards he is smoking by the open window. I look at him from the bed, where I am still lying with his sticky semen between my legs. He soon comes back to bed and gives me more nicotine kisses, and I think how easy it is to make love to someone when you are hungering as much as I am. I could probably sleep with anybody, but especially with someone this good looking.

It is August and there are just a few weeks left before we move to Stockholm. Benjamin and my best friends and I, all of us are moving. Moving to small student rooms in dorms where we have to share kitchens and bathrooms with other students.

We have only seen the rooms in a brochure but nothing makes us doubtful, because we imagine the great time we will have over there in the big city. There is not long left now; I have almost moved, home to Benjamin where I will find sanctuary and lots of love.

I work at a block of service flats during the last few weeks and I am struck with wonder about how happy some of the old people are and how sad some of the others. I decide to become one of those happy ones when I get old. That is why I need to escape. I wipe up shit and wonder at how incredibly long the old men's balls can be. More than a foot when they get to hang freely. Every night there is a party somewhere and suddenly the last weeks are over and it is time to leave. Benjamin has an old red Volvo which we stuff with our bags.

Mum cries when I hug her and Dad hides in the garage so I have to run there and yell 'Bye Dad!'

He mumbles back dismissively, 'Yes, yes, bye!'

It is autumn in Stockholm and I am so happy my chest aches. A liberating ache, a relief at finally, finally being grown up.

I spend hours in my green IKEA chair and think about how grand it feels to eat my own sandwiches for breakfast, with toppings I have chosen myself, soft cheese and pickles. I boil several pots of tea and fill my newly purchased teapot with Japanese symbols on it. It was expensive but it is beautiful and it is mine. I am happy when I see it on my little table and I drink hundreds of cups of tea in my room, which is over-heated with the twenty-four tea lights I have placed on every free inch of space. I enjoy sitting in my green chair and reading the books for film studies. Expensive, thick books in English which I do not understand, but I read them devoutly anyway and feel important.

Most of all I enjoy the solitude and the silence.

Benjamin wants to get together every day and every evening and I make excuses, saying I need to study, and it feels as though I am being unfaithful. Spending time alone is a new experience for me and I am confused by the fact that I prefer my own company to Benjamin's. It seems that I love wandering around in my own flat, listening to music, reading a book, cooking and most of all thinking long, uninterrupted thoughts. I get to know myself and realize that I rather like myself and my thoughts; that I am an OK person.

More and more often I feel that Benjamin is bothering me

when he calls and insists on coming over. Even more often I lie and say that I have a temperature and Benjamin becomes increasingly frustrated. I hear it in his voice and then I become irritated all over again.

One day a man comes up to me on Kungsgatan and says that he has seen me around a few times and would I like to have a cup of coffee with him? This is one of those days when I am exhausted and angry because Benjamin has called and insisted on talking half the night. I have grown tired of this kind of token of love, and during the entire conversation I longed to hang up and continue reading Deirdre Bairs' biography of Simone de Beauvoir.

I have just discovered certain things Simone de Beauvoir and I have in common, how her father started ignoring her when she turned eleven.

> It was never expressed in words and we were always
> polite to each other, but what had existed between
> us was gone. It happened around the time I turned
> eleven and ever since we've never got along.

When she turns twelve, Simone's father tells her she is ugly and from then on pays most of his attention to her little sister, Helene. I read and wonder what kind of life I want to live.

Those are the kinds of thoughts with which I am occupied, with which I want to be occupied. Now, when I have the opportunity to be alone for the first time in my life, Benjamin is there like a leech, obtrusive and slimy. Maybe that is why I follow this man to a café where we sit for hours and talk about life and our families and books we have read and movies we have seen. His name is Jesper and the conversation is filled with an understanding that makes me feel warm inside. It is evening and we go to a bar and continue to talk and I suddenly feel so happy I cannot make myself go home. I know that Benjamin has probably called seven thousand times by now and is wondering where I am, and I get angry when I feel that he is bothering me, that he wants to control me, that he is trespassing on my new life.

It is two o'clock in the morning before I finally hug Jesper and say goodnight and start heading home. Benjamin is sitting outside my door waiting, and I understand how angry he is when I see his fiery eyes set against his pale face.

'And where have you been?' he says in a low voice. 'I've been calling all night.'

He sounds like a father, or a big brother, or a teacher. The exhaustion wells over me, I am tired of feeling chased, tired of lying. I try and explain my longing to be alone and my meeting with the man on the street, but Benjamin just becomes furious.

'Are you crazy? You just followed a stranger and hung out with him until two in the morning?'

'Yes,' I reply, tired.

'And you only had coffee?'

'Yes.'

'And you want me to believe that?' he yells.

'Yes,' I reply.

'Are you going to see each other again?'

'I don't know. Maybe.'

'I'll be damned if you do!' Benjamin says, and throws my Japanese teapot to the floor. It shatters into a thousand pieces and I feel my body stiffen. That bastard. I sit down on the floor and start picking up the pieces. Benjamin throws himself on the bed dramatically, sobbing. His crying annoys me more than anything else because I want to cry too. Grieve for my Japanese teapot, my lost solitude, my forced coupling.

'You're walking all over my life. Do you understand that!' I hiss at Benjamin. He does not answer but continues sobbing. 'You're scaring me and I don't even know if I love you any more!' I continue coldly.

Benjamin stops sobbing and sits up on the bed. 'But I love you Sara! I've never loved someone so much before! You're the best thing that's happened to me! Please, can we keep trying? I promise I'll give you the space you need!'

I look at him for a long time, trying to invoke the sparks I felt the first time I saw him. I want to love him and my longing for solitude confuses me. Benjamin senses my doubt, a possible opening which helps him gather his courage. He comes over to me and pulls me down on the bed. Drenches my face in kisses and whispers things about love and the future in my ear and I am so tired I let it happened. A few days pass and the man from the street, Jesper, calls and asks if I want to meet again, but I say no. He sounds surprised and hurt.

'OK. That's a shame. I thought our meeting was special.'

'I did too. At another time I would have loved to get to know you better, but it just won't work right now. I am so terribly confused and I think I need to get to know myself first before I can start a new relationship.'

'I see,' Jesper says, and goes quiet.

I am burning with rage and I silently curse Benjamin's existence which makes me deny my feelings. We hang up and I curse myself because I realize that it really is not Benjamin's fault, but it is due to my own insecurity. My inability to have a spine. My need to satisfy people.

I put on my clothes and go out and buy a new Japanese tea-pot and stand a little bit taller. I make a promise to myself to try and be honest, so when Benjamin calls two hours later and asks if he can come over I say no.

'Why not?'

'Because I'm sitting here having tea and thinking, so now isn't a good time.'

'Stop it! Don't be silly, I'm coming over!'

'No, I mean it. You aren't welcome right now, I want to be alone.'

'To hell with it then!' Benjamin yells and hangs up.

I smile to myself and pour a new cup of tea. I am happy that I did not come up with yet another white lie in order to be alone. I put The Clash on loud and dance around and around in my small studio flat. In the end I am soaked in sweat so I tear off my clothes and get in the shower. I stand there a long time and let the warm water run over my body and I think about Jesper and Benjamin. Far off I hear someone ringing the door-bell. I turn off the water and listen to be sure. Yep, someone is ringing the bell and I think I know who it is. I wrap myself in a towel and go and open the door, where Benjamin is standing with a bottle of red wine in hand.

'You're unbelievable!' I say angrily. 'Can you not respect that I want to be alone and that there isn't a special reason for it?'

'No,' Benjamin says simply. 'I don't trust you any more.'

I fell silent. I understand him; I've been telling so many white lies that the truth suddenly seems strange. My guilt makes me let him in.

He quickly walks to the kitchen, takes out two glasses and opens the wine. We drink and Benjamin talks excitedly about his sociology course and the paper he has just started writing.

I sit quietly and pretend to listen but my thoughts run away to a slushy darkness deep inside me. Why is it so hard to own your life?

It is early spring and I am telling white lies again because I cannot manage to be straight with Benjamin. Least of all dare to admit that I probably do not love him that much, when he seems convinced that we are going to spend the rest of our lives together.

In April when the study grants have arrived for the last time before the summer, Benjamin convinces me to move into his teeny student flat. The timing is perfect. This way we get out of paying rent for the summer, and guilt ridden as I am about my confused feelings I cancel the contract on my beloved studio.

A week later when we are walking through Djurgården one evening, Benjamin suddenly says that he thinks it would be best if we ended things. I look at him to see if he is joking, but the expression on his face is serious. Embarrassed, he looks down at the ground as he is trying to explain. It turns out that he has been having the same doubts as me during the entire spring, but he was afraid that I would break up with him. Afraid of being left, he chose to be the one to do the leaving. Crazy with rage I curse my stupidity, my damned inherited insecurity. Curse that I am not fifty-five and life savvy, but twenty and stupid, stupid, stupid. Stupid and naïve and terribly deceived. I have been walking around for months feeling guilty about doubting our love while he had seemed convinced. So guilty that I even gave up my own flat because he wanted me to.

I start hating Benjamin openly. After a week he regrets it and wants us to get back together. Now it is my turn to hesitate, but it is only partially successful when we are living in a studio flat with a double bed.

Summer in that room becomes unbearable and I escape to Budapest with Sanna, manic and filled with sorrow and longing. Budapest is beautiful and filled with wonderful willing young men who want the best for us. We stay at cheap hostels where we fall asleep late and wake up heavily. We wander around during the day and float weightlessly through the city park's thermal baths amidst fat Hungarians playing chess at the edge of the pool.

When I finally come home Benjamin is wild because one of my benefactors from Budapest has called and asked for me.

'I know what you've been doing over there!' he hisses, eyes narrowed.

'If you only knew,' I answer with malicious joy, and bike off into the summer night to one of the countless picnics the summer teems with.

During the day I work at a group home and search the ads feverishly for a flat. Benjamin wants to go with me and he always finds big problems with the flats I look at. The rent is too high, ugly wallpaper, too far from the city, low ceilings. For some reason I do not understand, we always end up agreeing that it would be better if I stayed in his little student room a while longer. After all, it's so cheap.

Finally it is August and I am so unhappy and confused and desperate I decide to rent a tiny, ugly studio in an old service house from the 1960s. The flat's owner has been dead for three years. The management company has not noticed and her grandchildren have been taking advantage of the situation, letting the flat and raising the original rent by 2,000 kronor. But it does not matter, I will do anything to get away from Benjamin.

I move into the service house and I do not care if the other retirees wonder what such a young person is doing amongst them. There is one wonderful thing about the ugly apartment, a bathtub which I love deeply and passionately.

I take a long, hot bath every night while listening to Nina Simone cranked up loud and the dead grandmother makes herself felt via the antique lamp which is part of the furnishings.

I finally return to my solitude and my uninterrupted thoughts. Autumn makes the world reddish-yellow and I am taking an introductory course on literary theory. I make wonderful three course meals for myself and read strange books about Turpin in the *Rolandssången* and Brünhilde in *The Nibelungenlied*.

Benjamin calls once in October and sounds troubled. I am happy and chat and ask how he is doing and what he has been up to. He interrupts me and says that he is a bit stressed. He's just calling to ask if I can look up the word *cannibalism* in my psychology dictionary. He needs the answer for a project he is working on for sociology.

That is our final conversation and after that we do not see each other again for several years. From friends I hear he has a job as an *expert* at The National Agency for Education. He just went along there one day and introduced himself as an expert on student democracy – he has written a paper about student democracy and thought it would be fun to work there.

Yep, and here I become a bitter bitch again. I wish I was a man with inflated self-confidence who dared go looking for a job just like that, without any actual qualifications. Apparently it works, because he got the job and he has a business card which has *expert* written on it.

THE REVOLUTION WILL NOT BE TELEVISED

I woke up happy, every inch of me. Strangely enough my legs were sore but I did not have a headache. I took a long shower while humming the razor blade song. I giggled when I thought about the men's tongue movements, but stopped when I remembered I had booked to go on a hike in the mountains today. I hurried downstairs and gobbled up my breakfast.

I waited outside the hotel with a Finnish woman in her sixties for the bus which was going to pick us up. We start chatting and it turned out that she was from Åbo and could speak Swedish. Her husband was not coming, she explained, because he had recently had knee surgery.

'OK,' I said. 'What's he going to do today then?'

It was just a question, an ordinary one, but she snapped, openly irritated. 'I don't know. He'll just have to take care of himself!'

Enough is enough! That is the ticket. I laughed and said that sounded like a good idea. She softened up a bit and her husband came staggering out of the hotel to say goodbye or something. When I caught sight of him I understood exactly why she was irritated. He looked twice as old as her, and had empty, watery-blue Alzheimer eyes.

'Bye! Have a good time!' he said, while patting her shoulder clumsily.

'Yes, yes, you too,' The Åbo woman replied, irritated.

Her husband remained standing there for a while, looking as though he was waiting for something, a gracious nod, something, anything. But the Åbo woman had already turned towards me pointedly and started asking me questions. Why are you here? I explained that I was trying to write and needed to get away and be alone for a while. What did I do for a living? I said that I was a journalist and she brightened up.

'Oh, once upon a time I was a journalist too. But then the children came and there was no way of working such irregular hours any more. So I became a teacher. But I loved working as a journalist!'

The Åbo woman smiled at me and we talked about working conditions for freelancers; the uncertainty and the lack of money.

The guide and the bus appeared and we snaked our way along a meandering road high up into the mountains. Then we hiked down small paths for a few hours, through ancient bay forests with a fantastic view over the mountains and the sea.

The Åbo woman was content, walking with a small, secret smile. After two hours we stopped at a small bar in the middle of nowhere where the bus driver was waiting for us. Everyone ordered *la mumba*, hot chocolate with cognac, and the bus driver Diego immediately wanted to buy me one. I let him, he looked so nice and happy, so big and fat. An older Danish woman came up and complimented me on my baseball cap and complained that they had not put enough cognac in her hot chocolate. All in all our little group was very happy and energized by our walk. I thought about the Åbo woman's secret smile and about all of the human destinies housed in the little bar. And just in that moment it became clear to me that all of us are waging a battle for freedom in our own way. There are some events and situations I cannot ignore. Things I do not want to ignore. But maybe you can be a bitter bitch part-time?

I drank my pitch-black hot chocolate with cognac and grinned at everyone. Right then I actually did not feel like a bitter bitch. I thought about Johan and Sigge and all of the love to be found there. I thought about my unconditional love for Sigge, which is infinite and heals me with its greatness; my more painful love for Johan, which is also beautiful and filled with joy. Johan actually loves both my strength and my passion. Johan is the one I want to hold hands with when it is dark.

I thought about my friends who have saved me so many times, a kind of second family without which I would not have survived. I thought about my siblings, how proud I am of what wonderful people they have become despite our difficult childhood. And about how infinitely more boring life would have been without them.

I thought about my parents, Mum's love of life in the middle of all the hardship. A rough diamond. Dad's dark side, his grief and guilt which I have to find a way to live with somehow, and become reconciled with. I felt happy, melancholy, filled with love, rich and talented.

There in the bar on Tenerife I suddenly remembered an American documentary I'd seen about a man named Stevie. As a child he had been severely abused by his mother and placed in a number of different foster homes, where he had been loved by some but assaulted and abused by others. Now he was twenty-six and almost retarded, knocked around by life, walking around with big thick glasses, greasy hair and bad skin. His mother, grandmother and little sister all lived in the same community where everyone seemed to belong to the cesspool of the poor and unemployed. Stevie had contact with his biological family even though he was constantly cursing what his mother had done to him as a child.

In the middle of the film, during an interview about Stevie's childhood, it came to light that Stevie had sexually assaulted his eight-year-old cousin when he was babysitting her. His aunt, the child's mother, was heartbroken, but spoke the entire time about needing to be understanding because Stevie had had such a difficult childhood. Stevie's little sister, who was also Stevie's power of attorney, explained calmly that things did not look good for Stevie, particularly since assaults that he had made on her when they were children were listed on his record. Everything was mentioned in passing and it took a second before I realized the extent of what she was saying. Stevie had assaulted her when they were little and she was still worrying about whether he would go to jail. She was the family member closest to him, the one who took care of him, who allowed him to come along on holiday with her. She was at his side when he needed someone, and yet he had sexually assaulted her when they were children. My head was spinning and I grew hot and cold. How could this be possible? How could reconciliation be so great? These weren't people who had undergone therapy to survive what they'd been through. They had achieved all of the sensibility, all the love, all the reconciliation on their own.

There was a photo of Stevie as an eight year old, an incredibly cute boy with shy eyes, smiling and looking straight into the camera. The photo was like a reminder of who he might have been if he had grown up with love and not sexual abuse. And it was as if Stevie's little sister was constantly holding on to that image of him. In the midst of all the misery, all the horror, she never forgot about Stevie the boy.

And when I thought about her great achievement, I knew that reconciliation was possible for me, someone who had not been exposed to the assaults she had been through. Could I love and feel loved without ignoring or repressing all the damned injustices? Do I want to continue fighting and believing in change? Believe that it is possible to have an equal relationship? Maybe.

The bus ride back to our ugly hotel followed the same winding, meandering roads. The ocean lay below us, its infinity filled with promises. I turned and smiled at the Åbo woman sitting behind me. She gave me a serious look and took a deep breath. Then she leaned forward and stroked my cheek. Her hand was dry and rough and filled with tenderness.

I looked into her eyes. There was sadness there but also something else, something that had to do with survival and dignity. And there on the bus it came to me, suddenly and powerfully: a seriousness and a feeling of vital importance.

This is what life was about, the ugly and the magnificent. My life. The revolution will not be televised. Thank goodness. But it was time for a change. Otherwise I did not want to be a part of it any more.

MIDDLE OF THE NIGHT

Isadora is standing in her hotel room in Paris, alone and afraid, studying her naked body and trying to remember who she is. She pinches her nipple, studies her round stomach and the flesh on her bottom and thinks that despite everything, that she likes her body. Then she catches sight of her notes which are lying in a happy pile on the floor and starts to read what she has written.

> And then a curious revelation started to dawn. I stopped blaming myself; it was that simple. Perhaps my finally running away was not due to malice on my part, nor to any disloyalty I need to apologize for. Perhaps it was a kind of loyalty I told myself. A drastic but necessary way of changing my life.
>
> You did not have to apologize for wanting to own your own soul.

No. You should not have to apologize for wanting to own your own soul. But why is it so hard to be loyal to yourself?

Sometimes Johan asks me if I am living the life I want to live. I rarely answer that question. My idea of a happy life contains so many contradictory desires that it is impossible to combine them. I want to dance more, love more, be with Sigge and Johan more, work more, see my friends more often, maybe take a painting class? Spend time at the summer house we do not own, read more books, change the world, write, have time to listen to music, have more time for exercise, have time to relax, have time to feel good . . .

It is not that I am unhappy. My life is filled with moments when I feel pure joy, small torrents of happiness about the small and simple and fantastic, seeing Sigge running on the grass in the park, or seeing his concentration as he fills the bucket with sand. Feeling his warm body against mine and kissing his neck. Pure joy! And yet, if I look at the whole picture there is so much more I want, so much I want to change.

Isadora continues to read and realizes that she does not want to go back to the marriage she describes in her notes. If she and Bennett are going to stay together, it will be under new conditions. And if not, then at least she has learned how to survive.

She falls asleep happy and exhausted and wakes up when she feels blood gushing between her legs. She tries squeezing her thighs together but her period runs implacably in blackish-red lines along the inside of her legs, down on to the wall-to-wall carpet. When Isadora has finally found one of Bennett's old T-shirts which she uses as a makeshift pad, the room looks like a crime scene. It is time to leave Paris and get to London and Bennett.

I am reading this on my balcony at La Quinta Park. The sun has just disappeared behind the snow-covered top of the Mount Teide and an older man is swimming around and around in the pool below. He looks lonely and is swimming too hard, in a jerky, breathless way. It does not look as though he is enjoying his little dip; he is performing. I would like to give him a hug, teach him how to peel an orange. He could lie here and rest a while.

I suddenly realize that I should have had my period several days ago. I even packed some tampons so I would avoid waking up like Isadora with blood running down my legs. My period almost always comes early in the morning, sometimes in the middle of the night, but never in the evening or during the day. But now, nothing. One more thing, my period is never late. I go and pee and look down at the paper for a long time. But there is not the slightest drop of blood to be seen, just a little yellow pee.

I pour a glass of red wine and sit on the balcony and stare out into the darkness. I do not know how I should feel or what I should think. In any case, this was not the change I was thinking about on the bus this afternoon.

The old man has finished his swimming session and is sitting in his robe, looking out into the darkness too. An older woman comes over and sits next to him. He puts his arm around her and she leans her head against his shoulder. It is amazingly beautiful and I feel my emotions well up and run over. I want to experience that obvious comfort as well. Be filled with peace and calm. Be assured that I am making the right choice. The idea of another child makes me cry even more. It is much harder to start a revolution with a second child.

I cannot help but think about that grouchy old man God sitting up there in heaven, mocking me for having fallen for the most classic pitfall of womanhood, the one that gets women to give up and convince themselves that they are just downright grateful. This must be the punishment for my sunny daydreams about change here on Tenerife.

Fuck.

While I am crying I go ahead and let the old sadness over-
whelm me too. I cry for what has been. For everything that
became difficult and heavy when Sigge was born. It is still
tender. It still hurts. We were so helpless, we could not help
each other when we needed it the most. I need to move around
so I put on my trainers and my hooded sweatshirt and go for
a walk. There is a boardwalk with lighting along the seafront.
It is filled with people and I hope the darkness will hide my
swollen face.

Down at the beach I see a man in a Bamse Bear outfit standing smoking a cigarette with a large Bamse Bear's head under
his arm. He is probably working for the Swedish travel agency,
which has a family hotel with a Bamse Bear Club for the children. I stop for a moment and admire his seriousness, he is
standing completely still, staring out over the dark ocean in
thoughtful meditation. He is entirely unfazed by the fact that
he is dressed as a cartoon character, unaffected by all of the
people passing by on the paved boardwalk behind him. I want
to be that cool and self-confident, unaffected even by a ridiculous costume!

The cool evening breeze does me good and my thoughts
slowly clear. I walk for a long, long time, until my legs start
to ache. It is a pleasant ache that carries me away from all
the sorrow and towards reality. There is a pier at the end that
stretches out into the sea. I walk out on it and sit down and let
the waves splash drops of salt water on my face.

I wish Johan was sitting here now, holding me. I miss the
closeness, his body. I miss our conversations. All of the late
nights and evenings we have had during our eternity together,
when we have talked, about everything. Beloved soulmate! No

man has ever defended me so persistently, been so proud of me, so unafraid, loved me so much. Nor has any man hurt me as much, and disappointed me so infinitely.

The idea of a new baby terrifies me. I am afraid of ending up in the same chaos as last time. A few hours ago I felt convinced of the change that needed to happen, but I do not know if I have the energy to scream my head off a second time. I am afraid of being disappointed, afraid of discovering that we have not learned anything from our mistakes.

I do not know how long I have been sitting here on the pier but suddenly I hear voices coming closer. A middle-aged couple is walking towards me with determined steps.

'Oh dearest! You shouldn't sit here all by yourself!' says the woman, crouching down next to me.

'It can be really dangerous out here with the wind and the darkness! The stones get really slippery!' The man says, continuing to stand.

'It's all right!' I say. 'I mean, I'm all right!' My tear-filled voice probably reveals why my face is red and swollen. I know how red my face gets when I cry, even if it is just a few tears. Now I have been crying for several hours.

'Really!' I continue, when they do not reply.

'Yes, well, let us walk you back to the street, darling!' the woman says, and gives me her hand.

I take it and try and give her a reassuring smile, and she gives me a small smile back. They give each other a meaningful look and I realize they thought I was thinking about taking my life. I suddenly remember a scene from the movie *The French Lieutenant's Woman*, in which Meryl Streep stands on a pier just like this and is about to jump when she is rescued by Jeremy Irons.

It makes me laugh out loud and the couple look at me and at each other, worried. I need to try and explain; they are so nice and seem to want to do the right thing. I do not want them to worry.

'I was just thinking about love and life,' I say, trying to sound as calm and collected as I possibly can, but aware that it confirms their suspicion rather than relieving it. I cannot help but laugh again when I see their wide-eyed stares.

'I'm happy I promise you! It is just that I think I'm expecting another child and it brings back a lot of sad memories but also a lot of happiness!'

The woman is still holding my hand and now she takes mine in both of hers and holds on tightly.

'Oh dear girl!' she says, and looks me in the eye.

I realize that they are not going to give in, they really seem worried. So when they insist on buying me a cup of tea at the closest café I say yes. It was only a few hours ago that the Åbo woman stroked my cheek and now this. I wonder what signal I am giving off that makes older people want to take care of me? Maybe they see my longing?

So here I am sitting at a café in the middle of the night with a middle-aged English couple telling them about my life, and listening to their love story. It confirms every romantic cliché, their story is middle class and forty-six years old. She has been a stay at home mother to their three children and he is a doctor. The children are grown up and they have four grandchildren and they come to Tenerife for two weeks each year. Their names are John and Mary.

'Are you happy?' I ask.

John and Mary look at each other and laugh.

'Dear girl!' Mary says, and explains that happiness is relative and something you have to find within yourself.

John agrees and says that he is happier now than he was thirty years ago. Back then he was stressed out about everything that needed to be done, his career and the children. Now he is taking it easy and enjoying life. Maybe it is easier to feel happy when you're older, he says. Yes, maybe.

I ask Mary if she was bored as a housewife. She gives me a serious look and says that was life back then. Sometimes she was bored but usually she just enjoyed watching the children grow and develop. But if she were young now she probably would have done things differently.

'If I hadn't been a housewife I would have wanted to be a lawyer. Law has always interested me,' she says and explains that she studied law at the university when the children were older.

'Aren't you bitter then, about having to stay home instead of studying law?' I ask her.

She sits quietly for a while, thinking. 'I regret some decisions I've made,' she says, 'but I don't feel bitter. If I sat and sulked about everything I might have done I wouldn't have the energy to go on living. I try to reconcile myself with how things have turned out and make up for it by doing the things I didn't have time to do before.'

'But what you're saying now is exactly what I fear,' I say. 'I don't mean to be rude, but I really don't want to be sitting on Tenerife in thirty-five years, regretting my decisions! I want to make the right choices now!'

Mary gives me a serious look. 'Yes, but can you make the right choices now? If you can't, and there are many of us who don't always make the right choice, there's still no point in sitting here in thirty years feeling bitter! You have to learn to live with the fact that sometimes you're going to make mistakes.'

John is leaning back in his chair smoking a cigarette and looking out over the ocean. Maybe he is satisfied that he did not have to give up having a job and a career? Or does he feel guilty about everything Mary has given up for him? I am afraid to ask because I have already pushed the boundaries of honesty with my questions.

We sit there for a while, drinking our tea and talking about the trip to the parrot park John and Mary went on the other day. It was not worth the money, they say and smile at each other. John takes Mary's hand in his and she lets it rest there. And maybe the bitter bitch inside me is hiding in some crevice, because right now when I see them like that it makes me feel warm all over. I do so want to believe in their love. In a few rare cases maybe love can be true and still be this conventional and splendid?

John and Mary walk me back to my hotel and when we get there we give each other big, long hugs. They say that I must come and visit them in their seventeenth-century stone house in Windsor. I promise I will.

In the middle of the night I am sitting on my balcony, listening to the ocean. It is crashing and shouting and I cover my legs with the blanket I'm wrapped in. I am a bit cold but I want to sit here a little while longer and think about love, the myth of love, about equality and life.

And the children.

A HETERONORMATIVE
TWENTIETH-CENTURY ENDING

Isadora arrives in London and makes her way to Bennett's hotel and is allowed to go up and wait in his room. There she sees his jackets and ties hanging neatly in the closet, his slippers on the floor and his toothbrush properly placed by the sink.

She recognizes the sorrow in there being no trace of her having left him. A pile of theatre tickets shows that he has seen every play on in London. He has not had a nervous breakdown or done anything crazy. He is the same old dependable, determined, disappointed Bennett. And then she does the same thing I have done every night this week. She runs a hot bath. The best quick therapy there is.

> I hugged myself. It was my fear that was missing. The cold stone I had worn inside my chest for twenty-nine years was gone. Not suddenly. And maybe not for good. But it was gone.
>
> Perhaps I had only come to take a bath. Perhaps I would leave before Bennett returned. Or perhaps we'd go home together and work things out. Or perhaps we'd go home together and separate. It was not

clear how it would end. In nineteenth-century novels, they get married. In twentieth-century novels
they get divorced. Can you have an ending in which
they do neither?

It is my last day on Tenerife. I spend the whole day in a deck
chair by the pool, listening to country music and reading,
sleeping, reading, dozing, reading and thinking about Isadora
and her possible divorce. Yes, there are all sorts of possibilities,
for me too. I do not need to keep this child if I do not want to.
I can divorce Johan if I want to. I have complete freedom and
complete choice over my own grand, small-minded life.

The sun burns and I am sweating and I become happy when
I realize what I both want and do not want.

I *want* to have this child. I *don't want* to divorce Johan. I
really love him! Right now anyway, I am forced to add. I have
the freedom to make other choices next week, next month,
next year. But right now I realize that I am prepared to keep
fighting. I want to keep fighting. I think I have the energy to
argue and scream my head off one more time if need be. A
stubborn and defiant feeling fills me: I want to have my cake
and eat it too. It has to be possible.

I watch the young families around the pool. Today none of
the fathers happen to be drinking Heineken and none of the
mothers are screaming hysterically at their children, running
around the pool. Every family has their own group of deck
chairs which they have placed next to each other in a kind of
pattern of belonging. It is moving to see how they are lying
stretched out next to each other. Mum, Dad, children. Family.

The woman in the cock-coloured outfit comes wobbling
past my chair. She can also sit here with me and rest a while.

I feel for her, but today when I see her I am also angry. She sits at a table by herself a little way off and orders a bottle of white wine. Her husband comes a minute or so later with a tennis racket in hand. He stops at her table and says something to her before he walks off to the tennis courts. She looks down at the table, embarrassed. They are always apart and whenever they run into each other they do so with public contempt. I remember Isadora's words: you do not have to apologize for owning your own soul. You're right Isadora. It's your damned obligation. To own your own life.

Dear, beloved woman with the mouth of an alcoholic and the cock-coloured outfit, you have to get a divorce before you drink yourself to death! Your husband is not going to help you! He is playing tennis while you sit here alone and unhappy. You have to fix this yourself!

On the way back to the hotel room I take the path next to her deck chair. I want to say goodbye, and maybe something else, something about my insights. I want to say that I understand why she has become an alcoholic bitter bitch. There are thousands of valid reasons for every woman on the planet to become an alcoholic as well as a bitter bitch.

But that is the challenge, to keep fighting for dignity and for justice. The bitter bitch is just a consequent reaction against a sick system, a challenge never to satisfy ourselves with less than total equality.

The woman in the cock-coloured outfit looks at me and I slow down. I try and make eye contact and smile my warmest smile. I have stopped now. I am standing in front of her and I feel my warm smile freezing. She gives me a friendly smile but her gaze is distant. She struggles to maintain her position, her back is just a little too straight.

I am never going to despise grouchy women with tight lips
again. I am never going to use the word witch, because behind
every old hag there is a violated woman.

'*Auf Wiedersehen!*' I say.

'*Auf Wiedersehen!*' she replies kindly without having understood a thing; the look in her eyes is hazy.

'*Auf Wiedersehen* then!' I say again and quickly walk away.
I turn around and see that she is sitting in exactly the same
position, with her back a little too straight and her smile a
little too stiff, a little too unaffected. Is it going to end like
this? If so, it really would be unbearable.

In the hotel room I weep a little, a melancholy cry about all
of the unhappy alcoholic women, all the unhappy men swimming jerkily and playing tennis. I cry about love being so horribly petty. I cry because I do not know anything about my own
ending. I cry because it is so damned hard to own your own life.
I sit on the balcony and call Sigge and Johan. Today Sigge is
happier and he wants to talk. He has just watched *Bolibompa*
on TV and had ice cream with pears and whipped cream.

'Can you sing a sad song for me Mummy?' he asks.

'Yes, which one?' I say, even though I know which one he is
going to choose.

'The one about the herring,' he says, and I sing into his beautiful little ear, a thousand miles away, but very close to my
own mouth.

> Out in the deep of the Baltic Sea
> The little fish was swimming – he was so sick
> He had caught the flu under the ice
> He fought so bravely
> But he never came up

'Hello! Sigge, are you there?' He is quiet.

'Why didn't he ever come up?' he asks, as usual.

'He was so sick he couldn't,' I say, as I always do.

'But what happened, when he didn't come up?'

'Nothing. He's a herring, so he probably swam to his mum and dad.'

'OK. See you tomorrow.'

He gives me smacky kisses, right in my ear. I blow kisses back.

'Yes, see you tomorrow night Sigge!' I yell in a gruff voice, teary eyed as always when I talk to him. Johan comes back on the line.

'How are you feeling?' I ask. 'Are you angry, sad, indescribably tired or just a little happy?'

'No, I'm not angry or sad, just concentrating on work. Honestly I think you leaving has been the best thing for us. Otherwise you would just have been angry with me,' says Johan.

I know what he is like at the end of a project, silent and distant, or in his words, focused. That is exactly what I recognize in the eyes of the older men here at La Quinta Park, and that is what annoys me so much.

'I think we should do this every time I get close to the end of a rehearsal,' Johan says.

'What, I should go away?' I ask.

'Yes, I'm serious. I think it's great.'

That is exactly the glimpse of generosity which makes me love him, the feeling that he wants the best for me.

'But I've been doing a lot of thinking and there are things we need to talk about when you come home,' Johan says.

'I know. I've been doing a lot of thinking too,' I reply, and think about the new life growing inside me and the change needed if we are going to have another child.

We say goodbye, see you tomorrow. I miss you. Yes, me too. Kiss. Hugs. Goodbye.

I sit on the balcony for the last time and try and memorize the sun, the ocean view and the sound of the retirees, creaking as they roll around the pool down there. I will carry all of this with me back to the everyday winter of Stockholm. I will even carry the woeful women and their silent men with me; a reminder of how love can change.

The next morning at the airport I see Fear of Flying Girl with her boyfriend.

She sees me too and comes over. 'You're missing home, aren't you?' she says happily.

'Yes, I am,' I say, and discover that her question does not bother me. I really miss home, both Sigge and Johan.

'Have you had a nice time?' I ask, because today I am in a great mood. I am satisfied and proud that I have survived going away and thinking all of my long thoughts.

'Yes, but now my hell is starting. The flight, you know.'

She smiles secretively at me. 'I gulped down four whiskys at breakfast, hope that helps.'

I smile back at her. Then her boyfriend comes over. His face is sunburned, particularly his nose. He is fiddling with the gold ring in his left ear.

'Yes, my God, she's wasted and the plane hasn't even taken off yet,' he says and laughs.

I do not laugh with him. After a week at La Quinta Park I am tired of all of the distant men who hide behind their beer glasses and mocking irony. I am tired of men who are ashamed of their wives. I look at Fear of Flying Girl but she is looking at the floor. She is ashamed too, not of her nasty boyfriend, but of herself. The boyfriend is angered by my not laughing along with him. His smile stiffens.

'What the hell are you supposed to do when she's so fucking scared all the time?' he asks, without actually wanting an answer.

Fear of Flying Girl is still staring at the floor. Maybe she is used to her boyfriend talking about her with strangers in an airport?

'Maybe you should try comforting her instead of being so damned rude,' I say and walk away.

I feel my cheeks burn and I am sweating. Good God, what a reaction. I find a café far in a corner and before I sit down I make sure Fear of Flying Girl and her boyfriend haven't followed me. I order some coffee and a croissant and sigh with pleasure when the hot, strong coffee fills my mouth and burns my tongue.

On the flight home I can barely sit still. My legs are jumpy and the six hours creep by. My stomach is in knots with a longing that is endless. I try and read about Isadora, I just have a few pages left now, but my thoughts are many and they are all fighting for my attention.

It must be possible to love someone and still be their equal. It must be possible to liberate your life from the prison of patriarchal shit. Love has to be the greatest of all things. It has to be what makes change possible, what makes people want to do good. I am going to believe that. I want to believe that.

But then I catch sight of Joyce Carol Oates' words, a quote I have written in my notebook, which I often look at. Truth is desire; we want to believe; what we want to believe we call truth. And when love enters the picture we lose the truth.

I think about that. I think about the woman in the cock-coloured outfit, about Fear of Flying Girl, about Mum, about myself. I think that being quiet hurts just as much as fighting. I think about the fact that I really do not know what the truth is and what I want to believe.

My head is spinning and my stomach is filled with butterflies as the plane lands. A mild feeling of nausea spreads through my body and I chew frantically on my gum. Then we are there.

Sigge is sitting in his blue buggy with a half-eaten bread roll in his hand. Johan is crouching next to him. I had forgotten how beautiful they are in real life. I lift up Sigge and hug him hard and feel the tears start to come. I breathe in his smell, kiss his ear, his cheeks, his hair. I hold him a little away from me so I can see him properly.

'Hello my gorgeous little sweet pea!' I say.

'Hey!' he says simply. 'Why are you sad Mummy?'

'Because I'm so happy to see you again!' I reply.

'You can hug Daddy too!' he orders.

Our wise, sensitive child who constantly surprises me with how much he already knows about the frailty of love. I put Sigge in the buggy and turn to Johan. He gives me a questioning look and I raise my eyebrows and give him a questioning look back. We both seem to have a hard time deciding what mood should prevail – will it be the frosty sulkiness, the oh so familiar, which slowly but surely hollows out my guts? Or have we downright missed each other? My smile is a searching one. Johan responds with a slightly bigger smile. I feel myself grow warm and I take a step forward and he pulls me to him.

We kiss each other, a deep, long kiss, and I feel sparks.

At home all three of us crawl under the covers and we read *Gittan and the Grey Wolves*. It is almost ten o'clock and Sigge falls asleep exhausted just when the grey wolves are climbing up and getting stuck in the tops of the spruce trees.

'I need to take a bath,' I say.

'Do that, I'll come in a bit,' Johan says.

I let my body sink down into the hot water. I feel myself slowly relax and become warm. I want to read the last page in *Fear of Flying*.

Isadora is lying in the bathtub in Bennett's hotel room in London. She is waiting and wondering what she is actually going to say when Bennett comes in.

'If you grovel, you'll be back at square one,' Adrian had said. I knew for sure I wasn't going to grovel. But that was all I knew. It was enough.

I ran more hot water and soaped my hair. I thought of Adrian and blew him bubble kisses. I thought of the nameless inventor of the bathtub. I was somehow sure it was a woman. And was the inventor of the bathtub plug a man?

I hummed and rinsed my hair. As I was soaping it again, Bennett walked in.

The end.

I put the book on the wet bathroom floor and watch the paper absorbing the water, becoming lumpy and damp.

I see my body floating, weightless and warm. I run my finger over the bluish-purple scar from the Caesarean, from where Sigge, in another time, in a completely different world, was pulled from my body with strong hands. I wonder what Isadora's open ending actually means and realize that I strongly doubt whether their marriage will last, despite Bennett's entrance on the last page. Maybe it will last six months but not longer. Or maybe it is just wishful thinking, a compensation for my own Spartan ending.

Maybe it is like what Erica Jong writes in *Fear of Flying*, that you married in the nineteenth-century novel and got divorced in the twentieth-century one. In that case, I think, do you become heteronormative in the twenty-first century novel? It does not look better than this being a classic, heteronormative twenty-first century ending.

To my surprise this does not irritate me. I gently pinch my left nipple as I register this. I simply know that the bitter bitch inside me is going to make its presence known if I make a mistake. I run my index finger under my unshaved armpit and feel strong and determined, convinced about all sorts of changes that I *want*. I see my brown, curly triangle of pubic hair floating like an island of seaweed in the middle of the bathtub. I am happy there is no tampon string there, happy about the new life growing inside me.

And I am scared, scared that the carousel is going to start spinning again too soon. We just got off it, dizzy and ready to puke.

Johan comes in and crouches down next to the tub. He runs his hand along my cheek and I take his hand and place it on my belly. We look each other in the eye without saying anything and I realize that it does not stop here. It is a sudden and clear insight, a true revelation actually, that this crazy, disgusting, wonderful life is made up of crossroads. Not simple, often painful. But still, a number of chances to start again.

I guess life is made up of the grand and the magical, as often as it is made up of small-mindedness and everyday boredom. And then, when everything is unbearable, when it is January and you are distant and frozen, it is a matter of getting away to Tenerife for a week, or wherever, as long as you have the peace and quiet to think things through.

Am I living the life I want to?Never again am I going to apologize for wanting to own my own soul, my own life.

It begins now. There are no endings.

Thank you for the love and the friendship! Olof, Sonja, Bella, Carro, Daniel, Lise, Johanna, Kattis, Katja, Pål, Jonna, Anna, Micke, Inga, Claes, Lo, Karin, Jocke.

Thanks to all of those who inspired me: Nina Simone, Maria-Pia Boëthius, Hanna Olsson, Suzanne Osten, Gudrun Schyman, Carin Holmberg, Suzanne Brøgger, Märta Tikkanen, Susan Faludi, Kerstin Thorvall, Jane Fonda, Joyce Carol Oates, Martha Wainwright, Erica Jong.

Thank you to the Helge Ax:son Johnsons Foundation for the contribution which made it possible for me to continue writing.

Thank you to my brave publisher Eva and my devoted editor Tulle.